GHOST
TOWN

MYSTERIES BY JOAN LOWERY NIXON

GHOST TOWN

Seven Ghostly Stories

JOAN LOWERY NIXON

DELACORTE PRESS

Published by
Delacorte Press
an imprint of
Random House Children's Books
a division of Random House, Inc.
1540 Broadway
New York, New York 10036

Visit us on the Web! www.randomhouse.com/kids
Educators and librarians, for a variety of teaching tools, visit us at
www.randomhouse.com/teachers

Nixon, Joan Lowery.
    Ghost town: Seven ghostly stories/by Joan Lowery Nixon.
        p. cm.
    Summary: A collection of stories about eerie encounters in various ghost towns across the United States. Each story is accompanied by an afterword about the actual town on which the story is based.
    ISBN 0-385-32681-5
    1. Ghost towns Juvenile fiction. 2. Children's stories, American. [1. Ghost towns Fiction. 2. Ghosts Fiction. 3. Short stories.]
    I. Title.
    PZ7.N65Ge 2000   99-36340
    [Fic]—dc21   CIP

The text of this book is set in 13.5-point Adobe Garamond.
Book design by Susan Dominguez
Manufactured in the United States of America
September 2000
10 9 8 7 6 5 4 3 2 1
BVG

For my grandson,
Matt Nixon, with love

CONTENTS

WHO
ARE
THE
GHOSTS?

———·———

Hundreds of ghost towns are scattered across our Western states like dried, crumbling leaves after a winter windstorm. Thick adobe walls have weathered thin. Wooden posts and flooring have decayed. And even sturdy stone buildings have given in to the battering elements, their ragged remains marking the places where people once lived and worked.

Only a few of the ghost towns have been saved, their buildings repaired and painted so that visitors can catch a glimpse of Western life in the 1800s.

Most of the towns were established by miners hungry for their share of profits in the newly discovered veins of gold and silver. As time went on, however, some of these towns became hideouts for desperados. And there were a few in which groups of people attempted to establish other profitable industries and failed.

Miners, mountaineers, gunfighters, shady ladies, schoolteachers, preachers and their wives, workers and their families populated the towns. When the gold and silver were gone, the residents abandoned the towns.

Tourists from all over the world are not only curious about the Old West, but also fascinated by the stories behind each ghost town. Whether visitors believe in ghosts or not, once inside a ghost town, eerie feelings often engulf them. Just as sitting around a campfire listening to ghost stories makes you more aware of scary sounds, encountering a ghost in an abandoned town begins to seem quite possible.

Here are seven stories about real ghost towns in the West. Enter each town and walk its lonely streets lined with decaying buildings. See the shadows, and hear the whispers of those who seem unable to let go of their pasts.

These are the ghosts.

the
SHOOT-OUT

Chip Doby slumped in the backseat of his family's van. He wanted to be home in Phoenix with his best friends, Carlos and Dan. They'd saved enough from their allowances to spend all Saturday at the arcade. He'd saved, too, but a fat lot of good it had done him.

"Tomorrow we're taking a family trip to the town of Tombstone," Chip's mother had announced at breakfast on Friday. "We think everyone will enjoy a family outing."

"Tomorrow! But that's Saturday!" Chip's cereal spoon had fallen to the table, spattering milk and soggy Krispies across his T-shirt.

His little sisters had giggled.

"Sloppy, sloppy," ten-year-old Abby had chanted, while seven-year-old Emily had made a face.

But Mrs. Doby had said, "You'll love it." She'd beamed with excitement. "It will be great fun to see this historic Western town, and it will be painlessly educational, too. It was named a National Historic Landmark by the United States Department of the Interior back in the sixties."

Chip had groaned and dropped his forehead to the table, narrowly missing what was left of his cereal. "Tomorrow's Saturday," he'd said. "I'm supposed to hang out with Carlos and Dan."

"This is a marvelous opportunity, Chip," his mother had answered patiently. "You can walk the streets of the town, visit the restored buildings, and see the people in costume. During the day they even have make-believe shoot-outs. It's a wonderful look at the Old West in Arizona. Believe me, you're going to enjoy it."

"Enjoy national historic stuff? Sure."

"Charles, sit up," his father had said in a tone of voice that showed he meant business. As Chip had sat back in his chair, his dad had handed him a clean spoon. "And finish your breakfast. Your mother is right. You're going to enjoy the history of this trip. Tombstone is where the famous Gunfight at the O.K.

Corral took place, with Wyatt Earp and his brothers and Doc Holliday."

Chip had groaned again. "Dad, I can't go. I promised the guys—"

Mr. Doby had frowned, so Chip had turned quickly to his mother. "Mom, how long is this trip?"

"Only for the weekend," she'd said. "We'll be home Sunday evening."

"Then let me stay here alone," Chip had pleaded. "I'm not a little kid. I'm thirteen. I'm old enough to take care of myself."

"Out of the question," Mr. Doby had said.

Chip hadn't wanted to give up that easily. "Look, every week I mow Mr. Banks's lawn and ours, and last week I helped put a coat of stain on the backyard deck. You told me I did a good job. You said I was responsible. So if you meant what you said, then why can't I be responsible enough to stay by myself?"

"I did mean what I told you," Mr. Doby had answered. "You've proved to be highly responsible in handling the jobs you've taken on, but that has nothing to do with your staying here in the house alone. You're just not old enough, Chip."

Chip had looked at his mother. "Mom—"

"Our decision has been made, and we'll hear no

more about it," Mr. Doby had said. "Do you understand?"

"Yeah," Chip had mumbled, but he really hadn't understood. As he sat in the car, riding through southern Arizona, all he thought about was the unfairness of it all.

Off to the west lay brown, scrubby, low mountains and hills—the southern end of the Rocky Mountains that dribbled off like a gigantic brown lizard's tail. Ahead, along Interstate 80, which steadily climbed in altitude through the desert landscape, stood a few colorful billboards advertising the route to Tombstone.

As Mrs. Doby began reading aloud from her guidebook about the history of Tombstone, Chip wished he could plug up his ears. Instead he had to hear about some miner from a million years ago who was told that the only thing he'd ever get out of his property was his tombstone. So he jokingly called his mine and his town Tombstone. So what?

All Chip could think about was Dan and Carlos having fun without him at the arcade. They'd be playing Deadly Aliens, and he wouldn't.

Chip was relieved when his dad pulled into the parking lot and his mom's droning history lesson came to an end. But as Chip climbed from the van he stopped. "I heard gunshots," he said.

"That's probably a reenactment of the gunfight," Mrs. Doby said. She looked at her guidebook for reassurance. "We may have missed this one, but there will be another in a couple of hours. One is scheduled for two o'clock."

Emily's eyes were wide. "Who gets shot?" she asked.

"No one, sweetie," Mr. Doby answered. "It's all pretend."

"Come on," Mrs. Doby said. "Let's go. I want to see the Bird Cage Theater."

As they walked toward Fremont, the main street of the town, Chip hung back. He didn't want to see a dumb theater or visit the stupid old-time stores, which his mom was sure to do. "I want to go off on my own. I can take care of myself," he announced.

His words came out so loudly that his parents stopped and stared at him in surprise. Then Mr. and Mrs. Doby gave each other a long look.

"Okay," Mr. Doby answered pleasantly. He handed Chip some money and added, "Get yourself some lunch and meet us at two o'clock. We'll be on Fremont Street, watching the gunfight."

Without another word, Chip's family turned and walked on. Chip, who'd been ready to argue, stood without moving, not sure what to do next. He had a strange feeling that his family was glad to be rid of him. Well, who cared! They were the ones who'd insisted that he come in the first place. They were the ones who hadn't trusted him to take care of himself.

"You lost, kid?"

Chip hadn't noticed anyone nearby, so he was surprised to see a boy about sixteen or seventeen standing in front of him, his feet planted wide apart. The boy was wearing tight black pants, a black shirt, and a flat-brimmed hat that looked as if it had come out of a Clint Eastwood movie. Across his hips rode a gunbelt that held a pearl-handled gun, and the bottom end of the holster was tied with a rawhide string to his right thigh.

Chip blinked. "Wow!" he said. "Do you work here?"

Chip thought he saw a wave of sorrow pass over the boy's face before he squared his shoulders and answered, "You might say so."

"You're in the gunfight, aren't you?"

This time the boy's nod was emphatic. "Yeah."

"Cool," Chip said.

The boy shook his head. "Nothin's cool on a day like this. We need to get out of this sun and into some shade."

"Want me to get a couple of Cokes?" Chip asked.

"Nope. I don't drink," the boy said.

Chip laughed at the joke, and the boy added, "Steady hands, steady nerves. It's the only way to stay alive."

He led the way down a side street to a porch with a bench that stood well inside a pool of shade. He sat with his long legs outstretched.

Chip sat beside him and said, "My name's Chip Doby. What's yours?"

Raising one eyebrow, the boy asked, "Didn't anybody ever tell you it's dangerous to ask a man his name?"

"No," Chip answered. "Never."

The boy stared at Chip for a long while, then said, "You're a real dude, aren't you? Well, no offense taken. You can call me Billy. You on your own?"

"I'm with my family," Chip mumbled. He felt his face grow hot with embarrassment and hoped Billy didn't notice. Chip quickly changed the subject. "So, are you in the Gunfight at the O.K. Corral? What—"

Billy interrupted. "A lot of people get it wrong. The gunfight wasn't at the corral. It was on Fremont Street, down a couple of doors, in front of Fly's Photograph Gallery." Billy muttered something under his breath, then said, "Those no-good Earp brothers—Wyatt, Morgan, and Virgil—they thought they was runnin' this town."

"I thought Wyatt Earp was one of the good guys," Chip said in surprise. "Wasn't he a sheriff or something?"

"*Deputy* sheriff, runnin' for office of sheriff, and he didn't care what he did or how he did it, long as it would make people vote for him."

Chip was puzzled. "Like what?"

Billy winced, his eyes like slits. He slumped, his neck resting against the wall of the building, his hat pushed down over his forehead. "Like tryin' to wipe out the Clantons and the McLaurys after makin' 'em look bad . . . ruinin' their good names. He and that Virgil, who was servin' as town marshal, spread lots of talk about the Clantons bein' cattle rustlers, when they was just runnin' a few head out of Mexico. And then, when a stage got held up outside of Contention, Wyatt tried to make folk believe the Clantons were in on it. There was lots of stagecoach robberies that summer, and Wyatt and Virgil threw suspicion on the Clantons."

"That wasn't fair," Chip blurted out.

"No, it wasn't. Then for no good reason Ike Clanton got tossed in jail, and Wyatt clubbed Tom McLaury in the head with a gun."

"What did the Clantons do then?" Chip asked.

Billy sat up, pushed his hat back, and looked

Chip right in the eye. "You've got a family. You know how it is. Family comes first. Nothin' else is more important. So, no matter what, the Clanton kin had to stick together. So did the McLaury kin. They could either give up their property and leave town or stay and stand up to the Earps."

"What did they choose?"

Billy leaned forward, staring down the street toward Fremont. "They did what they had to do," he said. "They warned the Earps they were out to get 'em, and on October twenty-six, they met. The Clantons and McLaurys on one side, Wyatt, Virgil, Morgan, and their friend Doc Holliday on the other."

Slowly Billy got up. He stood with knees bent, leaning slightly forward, his feet firmly planted, his right hand poised over the grip of his gun. Chip held his breath.

In an instant, before Chip could blink, Billy's gun was in his hand, pointing toward the imaginary Earps on Fremont Street.

"Cool!" Chip said. "That was fast."

"Yup, I'm good," Billy agreed.

"With your job I guess you get a lot of practice."

"No doubt about it."

Chip thought a minute. "What exactly is your job in the gunfight?"

"To get that snake Wyatt Earp," Billy growled. "This time I will." He drew his gun again.

"Hey, take it easy," Chip said. He kept his eyes on Billy's gun. "It's only a reenactment. It's make-believe. That's all."

Billy stared at him, his eyes dark and penetrating. "Is that what you think?"

"S-Sure." Chip's voice was shaky. "I didn't mean to make you mad or anything. I guess you have to feel the part, being one of the actors. Right?"

Billy didn't answer. He slowly returned his gun to its holster, then checked its placement on his thigh. He squared his hat and stood tall, throwing back his shoulders. "It's time," he said. "Wish me luck."

He stepped off the porch and strode down the street.

Two o'clock already? Chip glanced at his wrist-watch, then hurried after Billy.

A crowd had begun to gather on both sides of Fremont Street. Next to Chip an elderly woman fanned herself, a man stuffed his mouth with hand-fuls of popcorn, and three shrieking little boys chased each other through and around their parents' legs. Everywhere people chatted and laughed while they waited in anticipation.

Chip felt a surprising sense of comfort as he caught a glimpse of his parents and sisters across the

12

street. *His* family. Emily was seated on Mr. Doby's shoulders, while Abby had found a perch at the edge of the boardwalk. He'd have fun telling Abby that he'd met one of the actors. She'd accuse him of bragging, but she'd want to hear all about it.

And wait until he told Mom and Dad that Wyatt Earp wasn't the big symbol of law and order they'd thought he was. So much for all that stuff Mom read in her guidebook.

An announcer introduced the reenactment, but Chip didn't pay much attention. He kept his eyes on Billy as Billy joined the other actors portraying the Clantons and the McLaurys. They stepped into the street, facing the Earp brothers and Doc Holliday, who had entered the street at the end of the block.

Slowly, carefully, the two groups of men walked toward each other. Suddenly gunshots rang out. The battle was on. Billy drew his gun with the same lightning speed he'd shown Chip. He was fast, but Wyatt Earp was faster. Billy suddenly grabbed his hand; it was dripping blood. He shifted his gun to his left hand, aimed, and fired, but the Earps had the advantage. They were too quick for him.

Billy dropped his gun, clutched his chest, and fell to the ground.

"Billy! No!" Chip yelled.

The man next to him turned in surprise. "Hey, kid, they're only pretending," he said.

Suddenly the gunfight was over, and the crowd began to drift back to the shops. But Chip ran to Billy, who had picked himself up and was hobbling around the corner. "Billy! You were great!" Chip said.

"Yeah," Billy grunted. "I can take care of myself."

As Billy leaned against the nearby wall, Chip grabbed his hand to shake it, but it was wet and sticky.

Chip looked at the red smear on his thumb. "What is this stuff, anyway?" he asked.

"Blood," Billy said.

"I know it's supposed to be, but I mean . . ." Chip stopped talking. He stared at Billy, who seemed to be fading away.

"Next time I'll get him," Billy whispered. "Next time."

Chip found himself staring at a blank wall. "Billy?" he managed to croak, but there was no answer.

"Here you are," Mrs. Doby said. She put her arm around Chip's shoulders, and he gave a start. "What's the matter, Chip?" she asked. "Are you all right?"

"*I* am," Chip said, "but Billy isn't."

Mr. Doby chuckled. "You must mean Billy Clanton," he said. "We saw the gunfight. The actor who played Billy was very good."

"That *was* Billy," Chip said in a low voice.

"That's what Dad just told you, doofus," Abby said.

"I mean the real Billy Clanton."

"Oh, sure. And I'm Doc Holliday."

Emily began jumping up and down. "I'm thirsty! I'm thirsty!"

"We'll all get something to drink," Mrs. Doby told her. "Chip, do you want to come with us?"

"Yeah, Mom, I do," Chip said. This was his family, and families should stick together—the way Billy had said.

"It's been fun, hasn't it?" Mrs. Doby asked. "It's not so bad to spend time with the family. Right?"

"I guess," Chip began, but he saw his parents exchange another one of those looks.

Never mind. He couldn't really explain his day. He'd keep Billy's story to himself. No one would understand. Not his parents, his sisters, or even the guys.

He glanced down at the red smear of dried blood on his thumb, and as he looked around the town, he knew he'd always remember this day.

TOMBSTONE, ARIZONA

In the mid-1800s, soldiers stationed at Fort Huachuca in southern Arizona thought prospector Ed Schieffelin was crazy. Trying to discover a rich vein of silver in hostile Apache country was bad enough. The dry, hot land was also a breeding ground for rattlesnakes.

"All you will find is your tombstone," one of the soldiers warned, and others laughed.

But Ed was persistent, and when he discovered the rich vein of silver he'd known must be there, he named his claim the Tombstone.

In 1879, as Ed, his brother, and other prospectors located more silver deposits, the town of Tombstone was established and began to grow. At first Tombstone was inhabited by miners, storekeepers, and saloon owners. But soon the population expanded to include gunslingers like Turkey Creek Johnson and Luke Short and lawmen such as Bat Masterson, Doc Holliday, and Wyatt Earp. With a population of around fifteen thousand people, Tombstone became a bustling town.

It was sometimes a violent town. A feud grew between a rancher named Ike Clanton and the Earp brothers, erupting in the famous Gunfight at the O.K. Corral in 1881.

The mines seemed to contain an endless supply of top-grade silver ore, but eventually water rose in the mines and couldn't be pumped out. Although Tombstone had been nicknamed "the town too tough to die," the closing of the mines forced people to move away to find jobs elsewhere.

In 1962, the United States Department of the Interior designated Tombstone a National Historic Landmark. Many of its buildings have been restored, and the town is open to visitors.

To reach Tombstone, which is seventy miles southeast of Tucson, take Interstate 10 east from Tucson. Turn south at the intersection of Highway 80 (Exit #303) and drive about thirteen miles.

To learn more about Tombstone, contact the O.K. Corral, P.O. Box 367, Tombstone, AZ 85638. Telephone: (520) 457-3456.

Web sites:
The O.K. Corral and The Tombstone Epitaph: www.tombstone-epitaph.com/

Tombstone, Arizona: The Town Too Tough to Die, Presented by the Department of Journalism, University of Arizona:
http://journalism.arizona.edu/tombstone/tombstone.html

———————•———————

Publications:
And Die in the West: The Story of the O.K. Corral Gunfight, by Paula Mitchell Marks, University of Oklahoma Press, Norman, 1996.

Tucson to Tombstone: A Guide to Southeastern Arizona, by Tom Dollar, Arizona Highways Magazine Publishers, Phoenix, 1996.

BURIED

"If there aren't any ghosts in ghost towns, why do they call them ghost towns?" Lauren Raney asked. She stepped out of the van into the parking lot of the visitors' center in Shakespeare, New Mexico, slamming the door behind her. The sound shattered the silence of the open desert country, and Lauren jumped a little, expecting someone to say "Shhh!"

"It's the empty towns themselves that are the ghosts," her mother answered. She waved a hand toward the dirt street that stretched out in front of them. On either side, past the sprawling old house that served as a visitors' center, were scattered an assortment of dusty red-mud brick buildings. "Believe me, I'd give anything to meet up with a ghost in one of these ghost towns. It would add a lot to my story."

Lauren's father had already pulled out his camera and was adjusting the lens. "The morning sun's just right," he said with enthusiasm. "I should get some fairly good shots of these buildings."

Lauren jammed a straw hat down over her dark, curly hair. With a mother who wrote magazine articles and a father who took photographs to illustrate them, Lauren was used to traveling. Sometimes she went to great places, and sometimes she wound up in strange ones. Ghost towns without ghosts were odd, and hard to believe. Those empty buildings looked as if they really needed ghosts.

An idea pricked her with excitement, and she smiled at her mother. "Do you mean it?" she asked.

"Mean what?" Mrs. Raney looked puzzled.

"Do you mean what you said—that you'd give anything to meet a ghost here?"

Her mother laughed, and Lauren said, "I wasn't being funny. *You're* the one who said you'd give anything to meet a ghost."

Mrs. Raney stopped laughing, but the grin stayed on her face. "I tell you what, Lauren," she said. "If you should come across a *real* ghost in one of these old mining towns, introduce me so I can interview the ghost for my article. I'll even pay you for it."

"How much?" Lauren asked. "Enough to buy my own computer?"

Mr. Raney shifted his camera strap to his left shoulder. "We've already discussed buying you a computer, Lauren. You're not old enough to need your own computer. Maybe next year when you're thirteen and doing more research for school assignments, we can consider it. For now you can use your mother's computer when she isn't using it."

"That's the point," Lauren complained. "When *isn't* Mom using it? She's always writing—even when I want to use the computer."

Mrs. Raney cocked her head and studied Lauren. "Okay," she said.

Lauren shot a quick glance at her mother. "Okay what?"

"Okay, I'll make an agreement with you. If you find me a ghost—a real one, not some make-believe thing—I'll agree to let you have your own computer."

"Marj," Mr. Raney began, but she held up a hand to stop him.

"Lately there have been a number of times when Lauren and I have needed to use the computer at the same time," said Mrs. Raney. "Maybe Lauren *should* have a computer of her own. We'll give her offer a try."

Lauren studied both her parents' faces, looking for a sign that they were taking this as a joke. "You think it's funny, don't you?" she asked.

"You asked for an agreement, and I gave you one," her mother said. "Isn't that what you wanted?"

"I guess," Lauren answered.

"Okay then. While we're here, see what you can scare up." Mrs. Raney burst out laughing.

Mr. Raney wrapped an arm around Lauren's shoulder in a hug. His deep chuckles vibrated against her arm.

Lauren followed her parents into the visitors' center. If she did find a ghost, they'd be sorry. She'd collect the best computer on the market.

Mr. Raney paid the entrance fee and was given a map. "Our tour guide will join us in a few minutes," he said. "I told her that while we're waiting I'd like to look around for possible shots." He led the way toward a two-story building.

"Shakespeare's a weird name for a town in New Mexico," Lauren said as she followed her parents. "What did Shakespeare ever have to do with a ghost town?"

"The town started out as a stagecoach station named

22

Mexican Springs," Mrs. Raney answered. "As it grew into a town it kept changing names. Finally the last mine owner named the town after his favorite author."

Mr. Raney opened the door of the adobe building, and the Raneys entered. Lauren found herself in a high-ceilinged room with plaster walls and a few pieces of rough-hewn furniture.

"This is, or was, the Stratford Hotel," Mr. Raney said. He glanced again at his map. "Next door is the Grant House Saloon."

"I've read about the Grant House," Mrs. Raney said. "There weren't any trees around here that could be used as hanging trees, so the Grant House, which had high ceilings, was used to hang convicted crooks and horse thieves. They'd swing from the oak beams in the saloon. There are still a few ropes dangling from the rafters."

Lauren gasped. "They hanged people right in the saloon? Where people came to drink?"

"To eat, too," her mother said. "Can you imagine stopping in for a meal and finding a body still swinging?"

"That's awful!" Lauren said.

"Let's take a look at the Grant House," Mr. Raney said, but Lauren shook her head.

"I'll stay here," she said. "I don't care how wild the

Western mining towns were. I don't want to visit the place where people were hanged from the rafters."

"But that might be the best place to find a ghost," Mrs. Raney said, grinning at Lauren.

"I imagine there are plenty of ghosts haunting this town," Mr. Raney said seriously. "You won't have to go looking for them, Lauren. They may even come looking for *you*."

"I'd rather stay here," Lauren insisted. Computer or not, she didn't want to face the ghost of some long-dead horse thief.

"Fine. Stay here if you want," Mrs. Raney said. "We'll be back to get you in fifteen or twenty minutes."

Lauren was glad to have her parents leave. For just an instant she wondered if there was any way she could create a fake ghost. Now that she was alone, she began to feel slightly uncomfortable. Maybe she should go outside. But the dry New Mexico heat was already increasing, and it was cool—even a little chilly—in the hotel, with its thick mud-plastered walls.

Lauren decided to forget a fake ghost. She couldn't jump out and shout "Boo!" to her parents. Instead, she wandered around to look into the other rooms of the Stratford Hotel. Stratford-upon-Avon was the town where William Shakespeare had been born. The person who named this place back in the 1800s must have loved Shakespeare. Her English lit teacher would have adored him.

As she reached the foot of a wooden staircase, Lauren stopped short, startled. She stared intently at a little girl in a long nightgown perched midway up the steps. The child was young—about five or six years old—and she clutched a large, beautifully dressed doll, pressing its china face into her shoulder. Lauren quickly glanced to both sides. Was someone trying to play a joke?

On the way to Shakespeare, Mrs. Raney had explained that a few people continued to live in the town, but Lauren couldn't help wondering why anyone would want to live in this old hotel. Who would let a child wander around alone in her nightgown?

"Hi," Lauren said.

The little girl leaned forward, staring at Lauren's face. "Emma?" she asked. "Are you Emma?"

"Where's your mother?" Lauren asked the child.

"Mother? No. I'm looking for Emma," the little girl said.

Lauren decided that the girl must have wandered to the hotel from somewhere else. Lauren's parents would return within a few minutes. She'd keep the little girl chatting until then so that they could help find her family.

"What's your name?" Lauren asked.

"Jane." The answer was barely a whisper.

Trying to make conversation, Lauren took a few steps toward the staircase. "Jane, may I see your doll?"

Jane skittered up a few stairs, farther from Lauren, and pressed her doll more closely to her shoulder.

"I didn't mean to frighten you," Lauren said. "Wait. I'm going to stay right here." She slowly sat down near the bottom of the stairs. She didn't know why Jane was frightened, but she felt as if she couldn't leave without putting the little girl at ease. "Tell me about your doll," she said.

Jane buried her head against the doll and hugged it in a strangling embrace. Again she spoke in a low whisper. "She's *my* doll! She's *mine*."

"I'm not going to take your doll," Lauren reassured her. "I just wanted to see her pretty face. I'm sure she's pretty, isn't she? My mother still has a china doll that long ago belonged to her grandmother. Maybe it looks something like yours."

"It's *my* doll!" Jane clutched the doll even more tightly.

Lauren smiled. She could see the back of the doll

from where she sat. To her surprise, the doll's white, ruffled dress was soiled with what looked like mud stains, and some tiny dried twigs and broken leaves seemed to be caught in the lace trim.

"Jane, why don't you ask your mother to wash your doll's dress?" Lauren asked. She pulled a tissue out of the pocket of her shorts. "Or, if you like, I'll clean her face and hair and brush off her dress for you."

Jane shook her head. She shifted, drawing her bare toes up under her nightgown. And, as she did, the doll half-turned slightly in her arms. Lauren caught a quick glimpse of an empty eye socket and a dark crack—or was it a streak of mud? For a valuable antique, the doll obviously wasn't cared for all that well.

She smiled at Jane and asked, "Was the doll a Christmas present?"

Jane shook her head. "It was Emma's doll."

"Is Emma your age? Is she your friend?"

"No. Emma's a big girl. I think she's eight."

"Did Emma give you the doll as a gift?"

"No. My sister Mary bought it from her with a five-dollar gold piece."

"Wow! A five-dollar gold piece!" Lauren said. "They've been out of circulation a long time. Where did Mary find one of those?"

Jane seemed puzzled. She didn't answer.

Not sure whether she was talking to Jane or to herself, Lauren said, "I think a five-dollar gold piece would be a lot more valuable than a doll. Of course, your doll would be an antique."

Jane's forehead wrinkled. Lauren realized that the child didn't know what she was talking about.

"I'm sorry," Lauren said. "Mary was really a terrific big sister to buy you that doll. Why don't you tell me *why* she bought it for you? You can trust me. Was the doll for your birthday?"

"There was a party," Jane answered in a tiny voice. "It was Emma's doll. She'd brought it with her from Virginia City. I liked the doll more than any doll I'd ever seen. I wanted it. Three days later I got sick, and in my sleep I kept dreaming about the doll and calling for it."

She paused, and Lauren asked, "Is that when Mary bought the doll from Emma?"

"Yes," Jane answered. "My mother put the doll in my arms, and I held it. It was mine, and I wouldn't let anyone else take it, or even touch it."

Two tears rolled down Jane's face, and she raised one hand to brush them away. "They thought I was asleep, but I heard Mary tell Mama that Emma wept when her parents took the gold piece and told her to give Mary the doll."

Jane began to cry in earnest, and the tears fell freely. "I wouldn't let go of my doll, even after I died," she whispered. "When they put my body in the coffin, the doll was still in my arms."

Suddenly Lauren felt colder than she'd ever felt in her life. Shivering, she backed up against the newel post, leaning against it for support. Her teeth began to chatter, but she did her best to speak calmly. "Jane, did you say you died?"

Jane nodded.

"Then why—how—are you here?"

Jane looked bewildered. "I have to find Emma," she said.

Still numb with fear, Lauren quietly asked, "Why do you want to find Emma?"

Sniffling, Jane said, "She wept for her doll."

"And you've been looking for Emma ever since . . . since you died . . . so that you could give back her doll. Is that right?"

"Yes!" Jane sobbed. She buried her face in the doll's stained dress. "Can you help me find Emma?"

"I'll try, and so will my mom. She'll be here soon, and—"

Lauren suddenly remembered the agreement about the computer. She *had* found a ghost. If she

29

could keep Jane talking until her mother saw her, the computer she wanted would be hers!

But that wouldn't help Jane. The little girl would probably be frightened by the adults and would leave. She'd continue to wander with a guilty heart, always searching for Emma.

Lauren could hear her parents' voices just outside the hotel. They'd return in a minute. She didn't have much time.

Lauren leaned forward, gazing into Jane's eyes. "You don't have to keep looking for Emma," she said quickly. "Emma was crying because her parents kept the gold piece and didn't let her have it. You were very sick, and she was glad to give you the doll to help you feel better."

Jane's eyes widened and her lips parted in surprise. "She wanted me to have the doll?" she asked.

"Yes," Lauren said. "I'm sure of that. She cried only because she wanted the gold piece."

"Lauren?" She heard her mother's voice at the doorway of the hotel.

"Are you sure?" asked Jane.

Lauren spoke quickly. Her mother would arrive in this room in less than a minute. "I know that Emma wants you and the doll to stop looking for her and to forever rest in peace," she said.

Jane seemed to smile. "Rest," she repeated. A little shiver trembled through her body. She hugged her doll tightly. Her shape began to flicker.

"Goodbye, Jane," Lauren whispered.

Mrs. Raney walked briskly into the room and up to Lauren. "My goodness, it's cold in here," she said. "It must be those thick adobe brick walls."

Lauren got to her feet, brushing the dust from the seat of her shorts.

"What a wild town this must have been. Come see the bullet holes in the walls of the Grant House," Mrs. Raney said. "Can you believe it? The men in the bar used to shoot at flies!"

"No . . . thanks," Lauren said. "I don't want to see them."

Mrs. Raney put an arm around Lauren's shoulders as they walked out of the hotel. "We didn't mean to hurt your feelings with our teasing about ghosts, honey," she said. "The idea of your hunting for a ghost was just too funny to pass up. Are we friends again?"

"Sure, Mom, we're friends," Lauren said. "But suppose I told you I *did* meet a ghost."

Mrs. Raney chuckled. "No more teasing about ghosts, okay? Let's talk about that computer. I think we can call it an early birthday present. Would you like that?"

"I'd love it," Lauren answered. She hugged her mother. "I need to do some research."

"On what?" Mrs. Raney asked.

"On ghost towns," Lauren said with a smile, "and on the ghosts who haunt them. What else?"

SHAKESPEARE, NEW MEXICO

Chosen as a stagecoach stop on the route to California because of a nearby freshwater spring, the tiny town of Mexican Springs soon grew into a busy mining town when veins of silver were discovered. Renamed Grant after then-popular General Ulysses S. Grant, the mining town was next named Ralston, after a wealthy investor in the mining district. Finally in 1879, the mining claims, including the town, were purchased by a British mining engineer, William G. Boyle. He named both the mine and the town Shakespeare, after his favorite author.

For a while the town boomed. But the railroad came to nearby Lordsburg, and people left

Shakespeare to live closer to the supply trains. Also, the mine's silver deposits began to shrink. The depression of 1893 finally forced the mines to close.

More than twenty of the original buildings are still standing. Visitors can walk the streets where prominent gunmen such as John Ringo and Curly Bill once walked and explore the Stratford Hotel, where Billy the Kid washed dishes. A number of strange occurrences and ghostly sightings have been reported in Shakespeare.

In *Ghost Towns of the West*, Lambert Florin writes about eight-year-old Emma Marble, who had come from Virginia City, Nevada, with her mother and sister to join her father, who had established a home for his family in the mining camp of Shakespeare.

Emma had brought with her a prized possession—an elegant doll with a china head. Emma took her doll to a Christmas party in 1882, and Jane Hughes, the youngest daughter in the Nick Hughes family, was captivated by the doll.

Jane couldn't stop talking about the doll, even when she became quite ill a few days after the party. In her delirium she constantly called for the doll.

Mary, Jane's older sister, visited the Marble home

and offered Emma a five-dollar gold piece in exchange for the doll. The request was granted.

Even in her sleep Jane clung to the doll. Soon she grew seriously ill and died. She was buried in the Shakespeare cemetery, where her body lies to this day, the doll still clutched in her arms.

Shakespeare is privately owned by resident Janaloo Hill, who has opened the town for tourists and conducts guided tours.

———•———

To reach Shakespeare, which is two and a half miles southwest of Lordsburg, New Mexico, take the Main Street exit (Exit 22) from Interstate 10 and drive south. Follow the signs on New Mexico Highway 494.

To learn more about Shakespeare, contact Shakespeare Ghost Town, P.O. Box 253, Lordsburg, NM 88045. Telephone: (505) 542-9034.

Web sites:
Shakespeare (with photos):
www.interart.net/travel/shakespeare/home.html

Publications:

Ghost Towns of the West, by Lambert Florin, Promontory Press, New York, 1992, pages 651–654.

Then and Now, Here and Around Shakespeare, by Rita Hill, Shakespeare Publications, Shakespeare, 1963.

"Shakespeare, the Town That Refuses to Give Up the Ghost," by Joan Marsan, *New Mexico Magazine,* Santa Fe, February 1998, pages 60–65.

the
INTRUDERS

"You don't know where you're going, Dub. Admit it. You're lost." Twelve-year-old Andy Karnes slumped in the passenger seat of the old pickup truck and glared up at his cousin, who sat behind the wheel.

"Am not." Unconcerned, Dub grinned at Andy. "I told you we were gonna take back roads up and over the mountains. Don't make no sense to run away on a highway where the law could spot us and pick us up easy."

Andy winced as the truck bounced over a deep groove in the dirt road. Studying the narrow ruts, he said, "This washed-out thing isn't a back road. It looks more like an old wagon trail." Once again he

37

wondered how and why he had hooked up with his sixteen-year-old cousin. Hadn't Ma said privately more than once that Dub hadn't been born with even a grain of common sense?

Sighing, Andy admitted to himself the reason he had involved Dub in his scheme to run away from home. Dub had wheels. Dub had this pickup truck. He hadn't been driving for long, but at least Dub was old enough to drive. If Andy had taken off by himself, he would have been on foot, hoping some farmer or kind old lady (hopefully not a serial killer) would take pity on him and give him a lift.

Mad as a hornet with a stick poked in its hive, Andy had broken down and confided in Dub on the way home from school. "I gotta get away from Mom and Dad and my bossy sisters telling me all the time what to do and how to do it. I'm gonna run away."

Dub had nodded agreeably. "Where you goin'?"

Because Andy had just come up with the idea, he hadn't thought it through yet. He'd shrugged and answered, "I don't know. Minneapolis, maybe. Or Chicago. Some big city as far away as I can get from Montana. I'll find a place to live and get a job."

Dub had laughed. "You're only twelve. You aren't likely to get a job."

"I can deliver papers or cut lawns or shovel snow in the winter."

"That's true," Dub had said pleasantly.

Andy had given Dub a hard, questioning look and had been glad to see that Dub was taking him seriously. He should have known. Happy-go-lucky Dub took everything at face value. Cautiously Andy had asked, "Have you ever been in a big city? I mean a city bigger than Great Falls?"

"Nope," Dub had said. "But I've seen Chicago on TV. I'd sure like to get a good, up-close look at the place."

"Then come with me," Andy had said.

"Okay," Dub had said. "Chicago's this-a-way."

Andy would have liked a chance to plan the trip a little better, to pack a change of clothes and maybe a bar of soap and a toothbrush, but Dub—who never seemed to worry about a single thing—had explained that he had gas money and they could always pick up clean underwear and toothbrushes once they got to Chicago. If they were going to leave home, there was no time like the present.

Andy had one more doubt. "I think we should tell our parents we've left," he said, "so they won't worry about us."

"You got your school stuff with you," Dub had

said. "So write a note. We'll leave it in your family's mailbox out on the road. Ask them to let my parents know, too. That'll cover it." He'd given a quick glance at Andy, who was already pulling a sheet of three-hole lined paper out of his notebook. "Don't tell them where we're going."

"I already thought of that," Andy had snapped. "You don't have to tell me what to do."

As soon as Andy had finished writing, Dub had said, "What did you write? Read it to me."

Andy had been about to tell Dub where to get off, but he'd realized they'd be traveling partners for quite some time, and it would be easier if they weren't mad at each other. So he'd read aloud, " 'Dear Mom and Dad, You had too many daughters before you had me, and you let them get too bossy. I can't take it anymore. I'm leaving home. Dub is with me. Please tell his parents he's okay. I know what you're going to say, Mom, but don't. See you when I'm grown up and rich. I love you, Andy.' "

"Sounds okay," Dub had said. "But what did you mean about that part where you tell your mom you know what she's gonna say?"

Andy had meant what she'd say about Dub, but of course, he couldn't tell his cousin that. He'd thought fast. "I meant what she's going to say about my running off."

Dub had pulled across the road and stopped by the Karnes family's mailbox. He took the folded notepaper from Andy, opened the box, and shoved the letter inside.

Gulping, trying to ease the tightness in his throat, Andy had given a last glance at his house, which lay some distance from the mailbox. Nestled among the wheat fields, it had appeared even smaller than it was—too small, with all those pushy big sisters living in it.

Dub had closed the mailbox, rolled up his window, and driven off, the wheels of the truck churning up clouds of dust. "Okay, Andy boy," he'd said. "We're on our way."

Now, as the back road grew rougher, Andy held tightly to his seat. "I don't know where this old road goes," he complained, "but I sure as heck know it doesn't go to Chicago."

Dub leaned forward, peering through the windshield. "We're north of Lewistown. I been there once. I think this road cuts through."

"Well, maybe it doesn't," Andy began, but he sat upright, gripped the handle of the door, and yelled, "Look out! Stop! There's a man in the road!"

Dub must have seen him at the same time, because he stomped on the brake pedal so hard only Andy's seat belt kept him from slamming into the dashboard.

The man was tall and lean, with skin just a shade more brown than the khaki shirt and pants and straw hat he was wearing. He nodded and smiled at Andy and Dub as he walked toward the driver's side of the car. Close up, Andy could see that the man was far from young—probably even a lot older than Grandpa Karnes—but he walked with long strides, his back straight and his head held high.

As the man leaned toward Dub's open window, he smiled. "Are you boys lost?" he asked.

"Nope," Dub answered easily, not the least insulted as far as Andy could see. "We're just cuttin' through."

The man shook his head. "This road won't cut through to nowhere. I don't know how you even found it."

"Are we still in Montana?" Andy asked.

The man nodded. "Just around the bend is the town of Maiden. This road dead-ends there."

Dub shrugged. "Is there a place up there to turn around?"

"Sure, but there's a paved road out of Maiden that

goes on to Giltedge, and from there to Lewistown. You'd be better off using that."

The man glanced up at the sky, then back at Dub. "It's getting late. Night comes on real quick in the mountains. Suppose you boys bunk here tonight and get an early start on your way tomorrow. I can fix you up with supper."

Dub looked at Andy for an answer.

The man seemed kind and friendly, Andy thought. He could practically hear his mother say, "Don't talk to strangers," but he was on his own now. He didn't have to take orders. "Sure. Thanks. Why not?" he answered. "We have to stop somewhere for the night. Might as well be here." Andy realized that the only cash he had was what was left of his lunch money for the week. Thinking of lunch made him so hungry his stomach growled.

The man stuck his right arm through the open window and shook hands with Dub. Next he waved at Andy. "You can call me Jep," he said.

"Hi, Jep," Andy answered. "I'm Andy Karnes, and this is my cousin, Wilton Haslip."

Dub spoke up. "Nobody calls me Wilton. They call me Dub, for the 'W' in Wilton."

"Just follow the curve ahead, Dub," Jep said, "and park your truck anywhere."

Andy clamped his teeth together as the truck jounced along the narrow, rutted road, but when they reached the clearing, his mouth flew open in surprise.

There before them lay the main street of an old Western town. Some of the buildings were built of unpainted, sawed lumber, some of logs. All of them were in near-perfect condition. A few of the false fronts that rose above the pointed roofs bore painted signs: Assay Office, Miners' Exchange, Bank Exchange, Berlanger General Merchandise, Drugstore, Feed Store, Jep Jenks's Barbershop—Caskets Made in Rear. But in the late-afternoon shadows, all the buildings stood empty. Not a single person besides Jep was in sight.

As Andy and Dub climbed from the truck, Jep strolled up to them. "You can see that you've stumbled across a ghost town," he said. "No one lives here anymore. No one but me, that is."

"You live in a ghost town? All by yourself?" Andy asked in amazement.

"Nothing wrong with that. I happen to like it here," Jep said. "I came to Maiden as a barber and casket maker and had a nice little business for myself—especially with the coffins. Lots of coffins needed. When the mines dried up and people left, I made my decision to stay."

"All by yourself?" Andy repeated.

"Look at those mountains," Jep said. "Ever seen anything prettier? It's always quiet enough to hear the birds talking to each other. It's real peaceful."

"No TV," Dub said. He shook his head in wonder. "No Nintendo. No Internet. No music."

Andy stared at Jep with admiration. "Nobody always telling you what to do."

"Yeah," Dub said, warming up. "No crime. No danger. No violence."

"Oh, there was plenty of crime and violence when Maiden was a thriving mining town from the late 1880s on into the very early 1900s," Jep said. "We even had to build a jail."

Dub looked at both sides of the street. "Where's the jail?"

"We didn't have it for long," Jep explained. "The carpenter who was hired to build it was so pleased with his handiwork that he went on a bender and tried to shoot up the town. So he was its first inhabitant." Jep smiled. "He was its last inhabitant, too. The next night, soon after he was released, the jail mysteriously burned down. People took it as a kind of sign, so the jail never got rebuilt."

"How did the carpenter take that?" Andy asked.

"He went on another bender after it burnt, happy

as a man could be, especially because no one bothered him. There wasn't any place left to lock him up in."

Andy frowned. Something didn't add up. "But that was a long time ago, and—"

Jep interrupted. "Far as dangers go, we've still got them, but they're dangers of the wild kind. There's always rattlesnakes, and at night bobcats come down out of the mountains, along with coyotes and badgers. Badgers can be mean if they think they're cornered. Best thing to do at night is stay inside."

"We can sleep in the bed of the truck," Dub said.

"You'd be out in the open," Jep said. "And nights get cold. You'll be better off sleeping on the floor by the fire in the main room of my cabin. It's nothing fancy, and dinner's only venison stew, but I'm glad to share it with you."

The sun had dropped behind the western peaks, and purple shadows were rapidly creeping over the town. Andy felt nervous. Rattlesnakes? Bobcats? "Thanks for your hospitality," he said quickly.

⬤

The oil lamps and the roaring fire in the stone fireplace filled Jep's cabin with a golden warmth. Andy stopped thinking about the scary stuff outside in the night and eagerly polished off the bowl of stew Jep set before him.

When Dub and Andy had finished eating, Jep put the dirty bowls on a sideboard. He quickly explained to them how to reach the paved highway that traveled to Giltedge and then on to Lewistown. "You can bed down early tonight and get a good start soon as it's morning light," he said.

Andy wasn't ready to go to bed. Dates were swimming around in his mind, and he couldn't put them together. "You told us you made coffins . . . caskets . . . whatever you called them," he said to Jep. "Couldn't people get them from a funeral director?"

"Funeral director?" Jep asked. He looked puzzled. "We had a minister who took care of praying over the dead when they were laid to rest in the cemetery. I guess you could call him a funeral director."

"But when—" Andy began.

There was a sudden loud pounding at the door. Startled, Andy jumped out of his chair.

Eyes wide, Dub was on his feet too, but Jep seemed unconcerned. He strolled to the door, opened it, and a large man in overalls charged inside. The man's hair, face, and clothes were smudged with black dust. He planted his feet wide apart, balancing like a fighter, and pointed at Andy. "Where is it?" he demanded.

"Wh-Where's what?" Andy replied.

"The lost mine. You may have found it, but you can't keep it. It belongs to me."

Andy backed up a step. "W-We weren't looking for any lost mine," he stammered.

"Calm down, Jim. These boys don't know about the mine," Jep told him. He motioned Jim to a chair, and when Jim had grumblingly settled into it, Jep explained, "They're on their way to Lewistown."

Jim continued to glare at Andy and Dub as though he didn't believe Jep. "It won't do you any good to find the mine," he said, "even though it's got the richest vein of ore in Montana. First man to come across it was Skookum Joe. He went down to Billings to file a claim, but he got to braggin' about the mine in a bar, and next day—afore he could tell anyone where the mine was—he was found dead."

"We're not looking for a mine, man," Dub said, but Jim's eyes narrowed, and he went on as if he hadn't heard.

"Soon after Joe died *I* found it." He reached into the pocket of his overalls and pulled out a handful of good-sized nuggets. He tossed one to Andy.

"You and your friend take a look at that," he said

proudly. "Pure gold ore. I carried chunks of gold the size of my fists out of that mine. Richest ore anybody ever seen. I showed them off at a saloon, and there was a rush of prospectors out to the hills like you never would have believed."

Andy examined the ore. It glowed in the light of the oil lamps, and it felt warm in his fingers. "Then the mine's not lost. You already found it," he said.

"I found the mine, but then I lost it again," Jim whimpered. His voice dropped almost to a whisper as he added, "Lots of men would leave home and families for ore like that. Take it from me, the hunt for the perfect ore gets in your blood. It possesses you. It makes you crazy. If the hunt for gold don't get you, the lost mine will."

With tears rolling paths through the black dust on his cheeks, Jim turned to Jep. In a pitiful voice he said, "Ain't that right, Jep? After I went crazy, everybody knew that the mine was likely to be stumbled upon again, but the finder was doomed to go insane—like me—or die, like Skookum Joe."

"Don't fret yourself, Jim," Jep said soothingly. "The boys aren't after your mine. As I said, they're on their way to Lewistown."

"The lost mine's cursed," Jim mumbled. "The gold . . . the mine . . . doomed . . ."

The door flew open with such a bang that Andy let out a yelp. "What are those boys doing here?" came a low wail. "They don't belong here. They're disturbing our peace!"

What was left of a man, dressed in miner's clothing, staggered into the room. With the one eye left in his head, he stared at Andy. Then he raised a miner's pick with his only remaining hand. "Get them out of here!"

While Andy and Dub gasped in shock, Jep stepped between them and the miner. In a quiet voice he said, "They're only boys, Zack. They left home, like we did once. Come morning, they'll be on their way."

Andy clung to the back of his chair. His knees felt so wobbly he was afraid he'd fall to the floor and never get up. "J-Jep?" he tried to say.

Jep didn't seem to hear him. He patted Zack's shoulder. "Sit down, Zack," he said. "Don't get so excited. It's not good for you."

Zack gave a long, hollow sigh. "Sorry, Jep. Ever since that mine accident killed me, I get upset easy." His one eye rolled toward Andy, and he scowled. "Some of the others hereabouts know you got company. Skookum Joe, Big Bessie, Press Lewis—and they don't like havin' strangers in this place that belongs to us." He sighed again. "I guess I should have waited and come with them."

There were more to come? Now Andy understood why the times Jep talked about didn't make sense. Jep wasn't alive now. He must have lived in Maiden well over a hundred years ago.

Andy cleared his throat and tried to speak more loudly. "Jep!" he said in a voice raspy with fear. "Your friends are all ghosts! And you—you're a ghost, too!"

Stunned as the room suddenly became dark, Andy slowly caught his breath and tried to stop shaking, "Dub?" he called frantically. "Where are you?"

"I'm here," Dub answered. Andy could just barely see Dub getting to his feet. "What happened?"

"You saw them?" asked Andy. "The ghosts?"

"You bet I saw them. Where did they go?"

Andy glanced around the room. The ghosts had left. Even the cabin was gone. Remnants of a cold stone fireplace and chimney were all they could see.

Overhead the sky was an overturned black bowl. Only a smattering of stars and a thin crescent moon gave light. A chill wind, swooping through the valley, made Andy shiver. At the close cry of a bobcat, he jumped to his feet.

"Dub, we've got to get out of here!" he shouted. "Come on!"

Stumbling over rocks and holes in the road, Andy and Dub raced down the street. When they finally reached the pickup truck, climbed inside, and locked the doors, Andy was still trembling.

Dub turned on the ignition and the headlights at the same time. "Look!" he said.

The buildings they had seen were gone. Only tag ends of stonework, weathered boards, and a few walls and porches remained.

Andy clung to the door handle. "Don't look," he said. "Don't even think. Just drive. Do you remember how Jep told us to reach the paved road to Lewistown?"

Dub nodded and lowered his foot on the gas pedal. "Straight ahead, turn left and then right."

A coyote's howl drifted down from the hills. Andy didn't talk. He scarcely dared to breathe until the truck bounced from the dirt road onto pavement.

As they picked up speed, he weakly leaned back against the seat. "When we get to Lewistown, let's not go to Chicago," he said to Dub. "Let's take the highway back home."

"Fine with me," Dub answered. "We can go to Chicago any old time."

"Yeah. Any old time," Andy said.

"What about your bossy sisters?" Dub asked. "What are you gonna do about them?"

"I'll think of something. I'll tell them everything that happened, and who knows? Maybe, for once, I'll be able to impress them."

"Haw," Dub scoffed. "You think your sisters are going to believe you? I hardly believe it myself, and I was with you!"

Andy unclenched his left fist and looked at the shining gold nugget he still held in his hand. He smiled. "Sure they will," he said. "I've got the proof."

MAIDEN, MONTANA

In 1952, while doing geologic mapping in the Judith Mountains, my husband stumbled upon the ghost town of Maiden, Montana. A few days later he brought me with him to meet ninety-year-old George Wieglanda, who lived alone in the town.

"This has long been my home," Mr. Wieglanda told me. "I had an assay office and mining interests in Maiden, and I like it here. When the others moved away, I didn't want to leave, so I stayed."

He told us some of the stories about life in Maiden, including the story about the building—and the destruction—of the jail. He took us on a tour of what was left of the town, describing everything so vividly I could easily picture how Maiden must once have been. Later I found photographs taken of Maiden in 1885 in the Culver Photography Studio in Lewistown.

Two of the mines in Maiden, the Spotted Horse mine, named after a friendly Indian chief, and the Maginnis mine, named after nearby Fort Maginnis, were heavy producers. Together they accounted for close to $10 million worth of gold.

In the late 1880s, the population of Maiden was nearly twelve hundred, and the town was prosperous. The first school was opened, as well as a Sunday school. Although there were a number of saloons in Maiden, it was fairly peaceful for a mining town and even had elements of culture: Maiden boasted the first cornet band in central Montana.

In the 1890s, however, the big veins were "pinching out," and rising costs cut into profits. Finally the mines were closed, and the peak population of twelve hundred people, which had been reached in 1888, began to dwindle until the town was completely empty—except for George Wieglanda.

Now the town is private property, most of it owned by the Wieglanda family, and visitors must get permission to visit.

To reach Maiden, take Highway 191 north from Lewistown, Montana, for fifteen miles. At a marked intersection, take the road east for ten miles.

To learn more about Maiden, contact the Montana Ghost Town Preservation Society, P.O. Box 1861, Bozeman, MT 59771.

Web sites:
The Montana Ghost Town Preservation Society: www.montana.com/ghosttown

Maiden—Montana Ghost Town: www. ghosttowns.com/states/mo/maiden.html

Publications:
Montana Pay Dirt: A Guide to the Mining Camps of the Treasure State, by Muriel Sibell Wolle, Ohio University Press, Athens, 1991.

Ghost Towns of the West, by Lambert Florin, Promontory Press, New York, 1992, pages 426–428.

PAYBACK

Alan Welty raised his chin and sucked in a deep breath of the cool Mt. Davidson air. The sky was so clear he could gaze across the valley below to the blue and purple mountains in the Stillwater Range. For the first time on his school's eighth-grade overnight field trip to Virginia City, Nevada, he began to relax.

Two tiny chipmunks scrambled out of the underbrush and rose on their hind legs to beg.

Alan pulled what was left of a bag of potato chips out of his pocket and scattered the crumbs on the ground. "Here you are," he said.

The chipmunks eagerly snatched at the chips, devouring them.

Almost hidden by the shadow of an old building, a small dog with mottled black-and-gray hair watched intently.

"Hey, boy, are you hungry?" Alan asked.

The dog remained still, and his gaze didn't waver.

Alan hadn't wanted to come on this weekend field trip. He'd pleaded a sore throat, but his mother hadn't bought it. He'd limped a little—even groaned—before his class boarded the bus, but Mr. Sands, his teacher, had just smiled encouragingly. "There's no need for you to miss the trip. Resting your foot on the bus ride should give it a chance to heal," he'd said.

Giving a hopeless sigh, Alan had climbed into the bus, taking a seat right behind the driver. He knew that his parents, his teacher, and even the school counselor were all in agreement that he hadn't made an easy adjustment to his new school. He could tell they thought he wasn't trying and didn't care, but they were wrong. They didn't know about the Tigers.

The Tigers were the three biggest boys, Bert, Harley, and Red, in Alan's class. They were all a year older than the others in their class, and they had banded together. Alan was sure they had only one purpose—picking out one kid at a time and making his life miserable.

Alan saw himself as an easy mark. New kid, unsure of himself, no friends to back him up.

"Hey, Mr. Sands! Better not tell the little kids about the ghosts in Virginia City," Bert had shouted as he boarded the bus. "Boo!" he'd yelled at Alan. "Ghosts in the ghost town. They're going to get you!"

Harley, following in Bert's footsteps, had jabbed Alan so hard in the shoulder that Alan had had to fight back the tears that burned his eyes. "Dead miners. Gunfighters. They'll all haunt you, Alan," Harley had said.

"Spooks! Watch out, Alan," Red had yelled, and doubled over in laughter.

Aurora and Georgia, who had been sitting near Alan, had glanced at him and giggled. "Mr. Sands," Aurora had asked, "are there really ghosts in Virginia City?"

Mr. Sands had smiled and shrugged. "I've heard stories of hauntings. But that's to be expected. Towns with exciting—even violent—pasts seem to generate ghost stories. I wouldn't let the stories worry you."

"Ooooh! Ghosts!" Georgia had said, and both girls had broken into laughter.

The Tigers had hurried to claim the back row just as the bus took off. Their frequent bursts of raucous laughter were as jarring to Alan as bumps in the road.

"Don't mind those jerks," the boy seated next to Alan had said.

Alan had turned to his seatmate with surprise. It was Johnny Wilson, the shortest boy in class. "When Harley laughed just now, you made a scrunched-up face like you just ate something awful," Johnny had said.

Embarrassed, Alan had mumbled, "The way my face looks is none of your business."

Johnny had just shrugged. "If that's the way you want it. I was just trying to tell you not to care about the Tigers. They gave me a bad time until they started bugging somebody else."

"Who?" Alan asked.

"You," Johnny answered.

Alan had scowled again as Johnny added, "They'll leave you alone, too, when they find another kid to bother."

"Passing them off to someone else won't help," Alan had told him. But in spite of what he'd just said, he felt a surge of hope that the Tigers might someday lose interest in him and bother someone else.

"You're right. It won't help. *Nothing* can help," Johnny had said matter-of-factly. "Nothing's going to change the way those guys act. Nothing and nobody."

"Somebody has to," Alan had answered.

"Right. Like you? Are you going to take all three of them on?" For a moment Johnny's eyes had lit up. "Do you know karate or something?"

"No," Alan had admitted, but he didn't say anything more. He didn't want Johnny to know that when Harley poked him in the chest, or Bert grabbed his backpack and threw it into the mud, or Red knuckled the top of his head, he didn't have the courage to stand up for himself.

Johnny had hung around Alan as their class began their tour of Virginia City, but Alan had slipped away from him and the rest of the group when they split for their lunch break. Johnny was a nice guy who was trying to be friendly, but Alan still felt new and apart and didn't want to work to make friends. He would rather be by himself.

He had wandered away from the main part of the town, past chipmunks fearlessly darting toward dropped crumbs of food and past the crowds of visitors touring houses, eating hamburgers, and heading off to explore the mines.

Finally he had stopped before the last old building on B Street. He leaned against the trunk of a sprawling cottonwood tree where it was quiet and peaceful. He gazed across to the Stillwater range and

61

gave a deep sigh. Somehow he'd get past the Tigers and through this school year.

Alan turned his attention back to the dog in the shadows. The dog's ears were pricked, as if he were ready to listen, and his gaze was steady.

Alan patted his pockets. "I'm sorry, fella. I don't have anything for you," he told him.

The dog continued to stare at Alan. His dark eyes didn't blink.

Uncomfortable at the dog's intent gaze, Alan glanced down at the chipmunks. He was so lost in the peaceful silence that he jumped when he heard Harley yell, "The one on the left!"

"Hey! What are you doing?" Alan shouted. He saw Harley pull back his right arm. "Stop!" Alan yelled.

A small stone whammed into the ground just inches from the chipmunks. Terrified, they abandoned the few crumbs that were left and vanished into the underbrush.

"You threw a rock at them!" Alan yelled.

"Smart guy. You figured that out, did you?" Red taunted.

"They're little and helpless. You could have hurt them. You could have killed them."

The Tigers laughed.

"Whaddya gonna do about it?" Harley asked.

Alan stared down at the ground. The Tigers laughed again.

Leaves crackled near the edge of the old building. Alan glanced in the direction of the sound and saw the dog take a few steps forward. The dog stopped, watching Alan.

The Tigers turned to see what Alan was looking at.

"There's a bigger target for you, Harley," Red said.

Harley picked up a small stone.

"No! Stop it!" Alan yelled. He jumped between Harley and the dog just as Harley let the stone fly.

It stung Alan's leg with such a sharp pain he gasped aloud. "Cut it out," he commanded,

"It's your own fault you got hit," Bert told him. "You got in the way."

Alan's leg hurt so much it was hard for him to speak. He took a long breath and said, "Anybody who'd hurt a dog is a stupid jerk."

The Tigers looked at each other in surprise. Then they grinned and began moving toward him.

"Want to say that again?" Harley asked.

Alan wanted to get as far away from the Tigers as possible. He was a pretty good runner. Maybe, even though his leg hurt, he could run fast enough to make it back to the crowd of tourists—and to safety—before the Tigers could catch up with him.

But what would happen to the dog? The Tigers were bound to take out their frustration on the dog if no one was there to protect him.

Alan stood as tall as he could. "Leave the dog alone," he said firmly.

To his surprise, the Tigers stopped. The grins slid from their faces.

Close to his side he heard a low, menacing growl. He glanced down, amazed. The dog seemed much larger than he had earlier. He was surely as large as a Lab. The dog stared at the Tigers, baring his teeth, and the hair rose on the back of his neck.

Harley took a step back. "Let's get out of here," he said.

"Stupid dog. He looks vicious," Bert said.

The Tigers turned and ran.

Alan let out a long breath. His legs trembled, and for a moment the earth seemed to rock under him. As he watched the Tigers racing down the street, he said, "Thanks, dog. Those guys are bullies. They would have hurt you. Someday they're really going to hurt *me*—unless I can think of some way to stop them. And I can't."

To his surprise, the dog was nowhere in sight.

Alan whistled, but the dog didn't return.

Poor old dog, he thought. *He's not vicious. The Tigers scared him so he's gone somewhere to hide.*

Alan looked at his watch. It was past the time his class was supposed to meet in front of the old Fourth Ward School. They were going as a group to visit one of the mines in the Comstock Lode. He ran all the way to the school.

Neither Mr. Sands nor the chaperones scolded him for being late. Stragglers were still arriving.

But Johnny came up to Alan and said, "I wanted to eat lunch with you, but you weren't there. Why weren't you there? Where'd you go?"

Alan just shrugged. He didn't want to tell Johnny—or anybody else—about the Tigers or the dog.

On the way to the mine the guide informed the class that Virginia City had once been the richest city in the United States, and that the Comstock Lode had yielded more than $1 billion worth of silver and gold. Gold had first been discovered in the Virginia City area in 1848, and the big silver strike had followed in 1859.

Intrigued by everything the guide said, Alan eagerly studied the opening of the mine into which they were led. Tunnels extended in a number of directions. The guide pointed out an old cage elevator. The miners had followed the veins of silver and gold, the guide explained, sometimes many levels down into the depths of the earth.

Alan found himself at the outside edge of his group. He glanced down the nearest tunnel, which was roped off and out of bounds. He shivered as he wondered what it must have been like to be a miner working for hours to carve out a passageway under the earth, with only a flickering headlamp to light the way.

To Alan's surprise, in the dim shadows of the tunnel he saw the dog with the pointed ears staring at him.

"You're squinting. What are you looking at?" Johnny poked his head around Alan, trying to see.

"The dog in the tunnel."

"What dog?"

Alan looked back at the spot where he'd seen the dog, but the dog wasn't there. "He's gone," Alan said.

"Whose dog is it? Where did he come from? What's his name?" Johnny asked.

Alan smiled. There was no way he was going to try to answer those questions. "He comes from around here, and his name is Comstock," he told Johnny. *Comstock. From the mine? Is that why I thought of that name?* It didn't matter, Alan decided. It was a perfect name for the dog.

Here, Comstock, he thought. *Come on, Comstock. That's a good boy.*

He thought about the way Comstock had protected him from the Tigers, and he wished he had a dog like that. He wished Comstock could come home with him.

During dinner that evening at the motel's restaurant, Johnny talked on and on about every single thing he'd done all day. And in spite of everything Mr. Sands and the chaperones tried to do to keep things under control, the Tigers laughed and shouted and annoyed everyone in the room.

Alan kept thinking about Comstock. The dog had such a strange way of staring, as if he could see right through skin and skull into people's minds. What kind of a dog was he?

Later, when Alan headed for the motel room he was sharing with Johnny, the Tigers suddenly stepped in his way.

Harley jabbed Alan with a sharp poke to his collarbone. It hurt so much Alan flinched, in spite of his determination not to. "We got something to talk about," Harley said.

"Yeah," Red said. "About those chipmunks."

"And your thinking you could tell us what to do," Bert added.

Alan took a step back, and the Tigers crowded forward, even closer.

"Boys! Time to head for your rooms. Lights out in half an hour!" Mr. Sands called from down the walkway.

The Tigers stopped and looked at each other.

"Okay," Harley said quietly. Jabbing Alan's collarbone again, he said, "We'll see you tomorrow morning. Early. You can expect us."

The Tigers disappeared as fast as they had come. Alan ran to his motel room, unlocked the door, and dashed inside. Quickly he dead-bolted the door.

Johnny looked up from the twin bed he was sitting on. "What's going on?" he asked.

Alan shrugged. "Nothing."

"Want to watch some TV?"

"Not now. I'm going to take a shower and grab some sleep."

"I guess you're right," Johnny said. "We have to get up early for breakfast. They're going to take us through the Castle and some of the other mansions. Do you know about the Castle? Have you seen any of the mansions? Do you know how rich some of those claims were?"

Alan didn't feel like talking. He hurried into the bathroom to take his shower.

He stayed in the shower so long that when he came out Johnny had fallen asleep. Alan wondered if the Tigers were safely in bed. He hoped so. For some reason he had a nagging feeling of being watched. Could they be lurking outside his door?

"Don't be dumb," he whispered to himself, but he opened the heavy drapes a crack to peek outside.

The parking area in front of the motel was silent, and no one was in sight. He decided that the motel guests must be safely tucked into their rooms for the night.

But across the walkway, just outside the small pool of light from an overhead lamp, sat a dog. His eyes reflected the lamplight's beam, and Alan could see that the dog was watching him.

Alan leaned forward, peering into the darkness. He recognized the pointed ears, the watchful eyes. He let the drapes fall back into place, snatched up his motel key, and silently left the room. "Comstock?" he called softly as he stood on the doorstep. "Is that you?"

The dog's ears seemed to perk even more sharply, and he rose. It was Comstock, all right, but what was he doing here?

Alan was surprised by how large Comstock seemed. He stood much higher than a Lab or a German shepherd. He was almost the size of a Great Dane.

Alan snapped his fingers. "Here, Comstock. Here, boy," he said.

As Comstock slowly walked toward Alan, Alan stretched out a fist, fingers curled down, so that the dog could sniff it. "Good boy," Alan said as he felt Comstock's cool breath on the back of his hand. He could tell that Comstock liked him.

Slowly Alan raised his hand and reached out to stroke Comstock's head. To his amazement, his hand moved through empty space. Comstock continued to gaze at Alan. He was certainly visible. Alan ran his hand along the space where Comstock's head and back should have been.

Nothing was there.

Gasping, Alan drew his hand back and pressed it against his chest. "You're a ghost! A ghost dog!" he whispered.

The dog's tongue lolled from his mouth, and he panted. He even seemed to be smiling.

"What are you doing here?" Alan asked. "Why did you follow me to the motel?"

Faster than a snap of the fingers, Comstock vanished, only to reappear across the walkway, where Alan had first seen him.

For a few moments Alan watched Comstock, and Comstock watched Alan.

A warm, happy glow spread through Alan's body as he realized what Comstock wanted him to know. Alan had protected Comstock. Comstock was now prepared to protect Alan. It would be payback time—in more ways than one.

Alan grinned. "We'll get those guys," he said quietly. The Tigers had no idea what they were in for.

"Maybe you could grow to be the size of an Irish wolfhound," Alan added. "Or a horse. Or a bear. Ghosts can be any size they want. Right? You could eat each of the Tigers—one crunching bite at a time. Maybe start with Bert . . . no, Harley. Start with that finger he uses to poke me."

Comstock wagged his tail. Again he seemed to smile.

Alan stood. "Good night, Comstock. I'll think of some more stuff before tomorrow morning when they come after me. Okay?"

The dog's eyes never left Alan's face, and Alan was now sure he could see Comstock smiling. Tomorrow morning Comstock would be at his side when he had to face the Tigers. Comstock had come to the motel to show Alan he was there for him, hadn't he?

Alan could hardly contain his excitement. Only he and Comstock knew that tomorrow was going to be the end of the Tigers and the beginning of Alan's real adjustment to his new school.

As he entered his motel room and again locked the door, Alan couldn't help laughing. Finally he had a solution to his problem. The Tigers would make a good meal for Comstock, and there wouldn't be a crumb left. Everyone would wonder where and how they'd disappeared. They'd search the mountains and the mines and never find them. He—Alan—would be the only one who knew what had happened to them, and he'd never tell. And no one would ever think to blame *him* for the disappearance. Alan didn't expect to sleep much that night. There were important plans to be made.

The moment Alan awakened the next morning, he ran to his window and opened the drapes a crack. Even though it was barely light, Comstock was sitting quietly across the walkway, waiting patiently. The dog raised his head and met Alan's eyes.

Alan raised a hand in greeting, then let the drapes fall back. To his relief, Johnny was still asleep.

Alan dressed and slipped out of the room and onto the walkway.

Quietly he waited for the Tigers to come.

He didn't have to wait long. Within fifteen minutes he saw them at the end of the block, ambling toward him. When they spotted Alan, they began to walk faster.

"Come on, Comstock," Alan called. He ran to the far end of the walkway and around the corner. There had to be an alley behind the motel, somewhere food for the kitchen could be unloaded. He and Comstock would be out of the way where they wouldn't be noticed.

He was right. His heart thumping, he saw that the alley was a perfect spot. The Tigers would think they had trapped him, but they'd soon find they were the ones who were trapped. He threw one quick glance over his shoulder and saw the Tigers racing after him.

Good! They were falling into the trap—just as they were supposed to.

Alan ran to the stained metal Dumpster at the end of the alley and leaned against it, breathing hard. He heard the Tigers pound into the alley and stop. He turned to face them.

Harley taunted, "There he is now, and no way out."

Alan raised his head and let out a piercing whistle.

"What are you doing?" Red stared at him suspiciously.

Alan leaned against the Dumpster. "Calling my dog," he said.

"Oh, sure," Bert said. He grinned at Harley. "You don't have a dog—not here, anyway."

"Yes, I do," Alan said. He saw Comstock move into the alley and silently approach. Comstock had done what Alan had imagined. The dog was massive, looming over the boys like a giant grizzly, teeth bared. Alan smiled. "My dog's right behind you."

"Oh, sure," Bert repeated.

"If you don't believe me, look."

Harley raised one eyebrow, but tempted to look, he turned slightly. "What? What's that?" He staggered back.

Bert and Red gave a startled glance at Harley and whirled to look, too. Bert yelled in fright, and Red backed up against the fence, as if he needed it to hold him up.

Comstock took a big step forward, his paws crunching heavily on the ground. The growl in his throat rolled like thunder.

"C-Call him off," Harley pleaded.

"No," Alan said. "He's hungry, and he hasn't had anything to eat yet. You're going to be his breakfast."

Bert gasped, and Red said, "Hey, we were just kidding around. We weren't going to hurt you."

"Yeah," Bert said. "In fact, we were going to ask you to join us. You can be a Tiger, too."

Harley began to whimper. "Don't let that dog hurt us! My mom would cry her eyes out."

"And my little sister," Red said. "She's only five. She wouldn't know what to do without me."

"You guys certainly didn't think about my mom every time you gave me a hard time," Alan answered. He wanted revenge but he felt uncomfortable when he thought about the consequences.

Bert took his eyes off Comstock just long enough to glance at Alan, and Alan was surprised to see a flash of what looked like admiration. "You're a lot like us," Bert said.

Alan stiffened. Bert's words came as a shock. A lot like *them*? Suddenly he realized he *would* be like them—even a lot worse—if he carried out the plans he had made. Was that what he wanted? Was that what he really wanted?

"Good boy, Comstock," Alan said to the dog. "Sit."

Comstock immediately obeyed. The Tigers stared from Comstock to Alan. "Will he do everything you tell him to do?"

"Yes," Alan said. "Now I'm going to ask you a question. Will you be giving me any more trouble?"

Their words a jumble, the Tigers shouted together, "No! No more! We'll leave you alone."

Alan smiled at Comstock and lowered his voice. "Thank you, Comstock. You're a good boy. You can go home now."

In one blink Comstock vanished, and Alan was left alone in the alley with the Tigers. He knew, as surely as if Comstock had told him, that the dog had left him for good. Comstock wasn't needed any longer. Payback was over. Alan was now on his own.

His heart began to race, but he stood as tall as he could. He thought about what Johnny had told him. "From now on you not only leave me alone," Alan said, "you leave all the other kids alone, too. If you want to bug anyone, bug each other. Got it?"

Harley took a step closer. The color had come back to his face. "You're telling us what to do again."

Alan took a deep breath. He felt good. "Yes, I am," he said.

Harley looked surprised, but Bert sneered and said, "All that big talk. Your dog was going to eat us, right? So what happened? Did he lose his appetite?"

Alan raised his right hand in the air, ready to snap his fingers. "Want me to call him back so you can find out?"

"No! Wait," Red said. He turned to the others. "I

don't want to see that thing again. Leave him alone. Who cares about him anyway?"

Grumbling, the Tigers walked out of the alley.

The moment they were gone, Alan leaned against the Dumpster for support. The muscles in his legs trembled, and he had to take a few deep breaths before he could stand upright. He'd never been so scared.

Alan snapped his fingers and gave a low whistle, but just as he'd expected, the dog didn't come. He'd protected Comstock, and Comstock had returned the favor.

"Thanks for everything, Comstock," Alan said.

But as he walked out of the alley, heading toward the motel, Alan began to smile. The problem of adjusting to a new school had suddenly become a whole lot easier.

VIRGINIA CITY, NEVADA

Close to the top of Mt. Davidson, Virginia City is Nevada's most famous mining town. Though the town has never been completely abandoned, it is still classified as a ghost town.

Virginia City once had a population of nearly thirty thousand people, and the nearby gold and silver mines were responsible for the establishment of many great fortunes. Quite a few prospectors, who came hoping to find rich veins of the precious metals, went from near poverty to great wealth when their claims proved valuable.

Virginia City is commercially operated. It has a visitors' bureau and a chamber of commerce information center on the site.

Much of the written history of Virginia City and of the huge Comstock Lode has been saved and is available to visitors, as are many relics of the mid-1800s. Mines can be toured, and many buildings—including some of the mansions of prospectors who once struck it rich—have been restored and are open to tourists.

At one time there were 110 saloons in the city. Now a few of them, including the Bucket of Blood Saloon, have been restored and are available for tourists to explore.

———————————

To reach Virginia City, drive south from Reno, Nevada, on Highway 395. Then take Highway 50 west to South Lake Tahoe. Virginia City is about fifty-five miles from Reno.

To learn more about Virginia City, contact the Virginia City Chamber of Commerce, P.O. Box 464, Virginia City, Nevada 89440. Telephone: (702) 847-0311.

Web sites:
History of Virginia City, Nevada, and the Comstock Lode:
www.vcnevada.com/history.htm

Modern Virginia City Scenes (with photos):
www.cal-neva.com/ghosts/ghosts05.htm

Publications:

A Kid on the Comstock: Reminiscences of a Virginia City Childhood (Vintage West Series), by John Taylor Waldorf, University of Nevada Press, Reno, 1991.

Ghost Towns of the West, by Lambert Florin, Promontory Press, New York, 1992, pages 595–596.

the MAGIC EYE

Ashley Banks tugged at the full, heavy skirt of her costume. "It's too tight at the waist," she complained.

Mrs. Dacy, on her knees in the motel conference room designated as the wardrobe department, shrugged and ran her fingers through her orange-red hair.

"Get used to it," she said. "They wore 'em tight—corsets and all—back in the 1800s. Even the little kids like you."

Ashley rolled her eyes. "I'm not a little kid, Mrs. Dacy," she said. She shoved her hands into the pockets of the skirt, touching the weird little stone she had found earlier. "I'm fourteen, and I wish this costume fit better."

Suddenly, to Ashley's surprise, the waistline eased. "There you go," Mrs. Dacy said. "I found two darts basted in and pulled the threads. Better?"

"Yes. Thank you," Ashley answered. She laughed. "I guess wishes *do* come true." Was it her imagination, or did the stone feel warm to her touch? Glancing into the full-length mirror before she removed the dress, she realized just how becoming the dress was. The faded blue cotton print made her eyes seem even bluer than usual and set off the spirals of blond hair that framed her face.

Ashley still couldn't believe she was going to be in a real movie, even if it wasn't a big role. Word had spread that a Hollywood company would be shooting a film on a set constructed in the ghost town of Grafton. Kids of all ages who lived in southern Utah had been invited to audition for parts as extras.

Being picked was pure luck, Ashley cheerfully reminded herself. And luck was something she never stopped looking for. Rabbits' feet, shamrocks, horseshoes—Ashley had tried all of them, and she was convinced they worked. Now she had found a stone that seemed to bring good luck. Hadn't her dress immediately felt better as soon as she'd wished it would? She took the stone from the pocket of the costume. Looking at it again, she realized how strange it was.

It was small, oval, and as smooth as glass. What made it truly unusual though, were its deep red, yellow, and white markings, which resembled a wide-open eye.

The night before, as Ashley and her mother had climbed into their twin beds in the motel near St. George, Ashley had placed the stone on the table between their beds.

"Where did you get that thing?" her mother had asked. "It looks like it's staring at me. It's creepy."

Ashley had giggled. "It was in the cemetery."

"What?"

"Really, Mom. I found it between rehearsals yesterday, when I was looking around the old ghost town. The stone must have been lying right next to a tombstone. It rolled against my shoe like a gift. As if someone wanted me to have it."

Mrs. Banks had shivered. "If I were you, I'd give it back."

"No. I'm going to keep it," Ashley had answered. "It's so weird it must be lucky." She had reached to turn off the light.

"That's just wishful thinking. People make their own luck, not charms." her mother had grumbled. She'd rolled onto her side, pulling the thin blanket and sheet up to her ears.

Ashley didn't give another thought to her mother's opinion. She had touched the stone, made a wish, and her dress suddenly fit. Didn't that prove she had found a lucky stone? It was more than lucky. It had to be magic.

Now, as she placed the stone in the pocket of her jeans, she once more felt a strange excitement. Something interesting was bound to happen to the owner of a stone like this one.

A few steps down and across the hall from the wardrobe department, a door stood open. Ashley paused to glance inside the room, which was cluttered with odds and ends that were surely movie props. Who else would want a moth-eaten bear rug, two Indian war bonnets, a bunch of spears, and a pile of worn saddles?

She lifted her gaze to the wall at her right and gasped aloud. There, in a cheap, tarnished frame, was a photograph of the best-looking boy she had ever seen.

Even though the black-and-white print was grainy, it couldn't disguise high cheekbones, a strong, square chin, and dark eyes that seemed to stare right into her own. A broad-brimmed felt hat was pushed back on the boy's head, and long gleaming black hair skimmed the collar of his denim shirt. Under his collar hung the rawhide strip of a bolo tie. It was fastened with a scrolled silver clasp set with polished blue chips that looked like turquoise.

Entranced, Ashley gripped the stone in her pocket as she stared at the photo. The boy must be somewhere between sixteen and eighteen, and he certainly looked like a star. *I wonder if he's in this film, too,* she thought. In her mind she spoke to the face in the photograph. *I wish I could meet you.*

She smiled as she suddenly imagined the two of them, alone under the stars. He'd put an arm around her shoulders, and his lips would lightly touch hers . . . "I wish," she whispered.

"What are you smiling about?"

Ashley whirled around. There sat the boy in the photograph. He was perched on a stack of large cardboard boxes, grinning at her.

"N-Nothing really," Ashley stammered. "That is . . . I mean . . . I was looking at your photograph, and I wondered—" She felt herself blush. "I wondered if you were cast in the movie, too."

She almost groaned aloud. Why couldn't she talk straight or make sense? And why hadn't she said "film" instead of "movie"? She'd sounded so dumb.

But the boy said, "Hi. I'm Luke Danvers. And you're Ashley Banks." His broad smile nearly took Ashley's breath away.

"How did you know my name?"

"Easy. The studio people take roll call every time they go out on location."

"Oh. Of course." Desperately searching for something to talk about, Ashley blurted out, "Do you know what the film is about? I haven't seen a script. The casting director said extras wouldn't need one. We'd be told what to do."

She stopped, embarrassed again, but Luke seemed interested in her question.

"They're making what they call a classic Western," he said. "You know—settlers against the spring floods and the uprisings of the Native Americans."

His eyes seemed to grow darker and deeper. "The Hollywood people who make films don't think about the deeper issues. They probably don't know or care that this land once belonged to many tribes—like the Shoshones and the Paiutes."

As he spoke, Luke's voice grew angrier. "The land the Mormon settlers named Zion has been a hallowed place for centuries, rich with spirits. For many years young warriors and wise elders came into the mountains to meditate and talk to the gods. Then white settlers arrived and claimed the land, which was not theirs to take."

Luke stopped speaking for a moment. Then he

went on, his anger seemingly under control. "You've seen the rugged peak of Mount Kinesava, which towers over the town of Grafton?"

Ashley nodded. "It's part of Zion."

"It's part of a temple. That land was mystical. It still is, even though the settlers interfered."

"But the settlers left."

"Those who were still alive." Luke's voice dropped so low that Ashley could scarcely hear it. "Many of them are still there. The tombstones in the cemetery at Grafton mark countless graves of settlers who died in the tribal raids and who tried to flee the Blackhawk War."

Ashley pictured the cemetery and the jagged red-and-gold peaks that rose above it, the town and mountain separated only by the Virgin River, which twisted between them. "The mystical land, the spirits, are they still there, too?" she asked.

"Yes." Luke nodded. "Let me try to explain. There are certain places in this world that are attuned to both the inner and outer forces of the earth. The Zion peaks are among them. They're a channel through which great magic can take place."

"What kind of magic?"

An impatient voice shouted down the hallway, "Ashley Banks! Where are you? Report at once to Makeup!"

"Don't go," Luke said. "Come with me. I'll show you."

Reluctantly Ashley answered, "I wish I could, but I have to report to Makeup."

She ran into the hallway, almost colliding with an older woman, who pressed against the wall to get out of Ashley's way.

"Ooops! I'm sorry," Ashley said. She put out a hand to steady the woman.

Stepping away from the wall, the woman shook her head. She was short and small-boned, with deeply tanned skin, and her long gray hair was fastened at the nape of her neck with a rubber band. "Young people are so impatient," she said. "Where were you rushing off to so fast?"

"To Makeup," Ashley answered. "I'm in this movie—uh, film—they're making. Oh, I'm sorry. I suppose you are, too."

"Me? Oh, no," the woman said. "I'm Maria Blanton. I own this motel, but my son, Anthony, runs it. Why I rented it out to a movie company, I don't know. Well, I do know. A full house means money in the bank."

"Yes, Mrs. Blanton," Ashley said. She tried to edge past the woman, but Mrs. Blanton didn't seem to be finished with what she had to say.

"Those Hollywood people film around Grafton every so often. Sometimes people in the movie companies stay here. Robert Redford and Paul Newman once made a movie here. Big stars. It's different now. I don't know the Hollywood people in this movie. I never go to the movies anymore."

"Yes, ma'am," Ashley said. She managed to squeeze around Mrs. Blanton and hurry into the room with the Makeup sign tacked to the door.

Half an hour later Ashley gave her name to a woman with a clipboard and climbed on the bus that would take the extras to the set. She checked the seats carefully and realized, to her disappointment, that Luke Danvers wasn't aboard.

But when the bus reached the set, lumbering to a stop behind a line of buses already parked, Ashley saw Luke from the window. He was standing near the river, with Mount Kinesava rising up like a hovering giant behind him. *Let him be waiting for me*, Ashley hoped. *I wish I could get to know him better.*

With a start, Ashley saw that Luke's eyes were fixed on hers. He smiled and raised a hand, beckoning.

Ashley scrambled out of her seat and hurried to get off the bus.

Luke approached her, holding out a hand. "Come with me," he said.

Ashley glanced around the parking lot. The other extras were making their way toward the set. "Come where?" she asked.

Luke grinned. "To the magical mountains," he said.

"Now?"

"Now."

"Ashley!" a voice called.

Ashley glanced over her shoulder and saw the studio teacher, Ms. Dunn, motioning to her.

"This way, please. They've set up a trailer for our classroom. The others are already there."

"Later," Ashley quickly told Luke. She ran to catch up with Ms. Dunn.

Ms. Dunn smiled pleasantly, but she said, "Each morning you're supposed to report to me. Where were you off to?"

"To the magic—to the mountains," Ashley answered.

Ms. Dunn looked concerned. "Haven't you been given the warnings?" she asked.

"What warnings?" A shiver trembled along Ashley's spine. Putting her hands in her pockets, she reached for the comfort of her magic stone, but it felt so cold and hard that she quickly pulled her fingers away.

"It's easy to get lost in those mountains," Ms. Dunn said. "No one should hike into them alone. People have disappeared and never been found."

But I'd be with Luke, Ashley thought. *I'd be perfectly safe.*

However, she did as she was told. The day was taken up with classroom work, rehearsal, and a lot of waiting. Lights were set up. Lights were taken down. Props were arranged and rearranged. Moviemaking was incredibly boring, Ashley decided.

During the afternoon, gray clouds gathered, and the mountain peaks darkened in their shadow. Now and then Sam, the director, squinted up at the sky. "The clouds look good," he said to one of his assistants. "They're just what we want, as long as they don't turn into rainstorms, delay filming, and wreck the budget."

"Don't worry so much," the assistant answered. "The TV weatherman said it's not going to rain. You wanted clouds, and that's what you got."

Ashley looked for Luke, but he was nowhere in sight.

It wasn't until she was back at the motel, walking down the hallway toward the room she shared with her mother, that she heard Luke's voice. He called to her from the storeroom, where once again he was perched on the pile of boxes.

Ashley glanced through the open doorway at Luke's handsome face, and her heart jumped with happiness.

"You didn't come with me," he said.

He wasn't scolding. His smile was soft and warm, so Ashley relaxed and smiled back. "You know I couldn't."

"You could have if you'd wanted to. You made a wish. Wishes, once granted, must be carried out."

Ashley was puzzled. She couldn't remember making any wishes out loud. And he couldn't know about the wishes she'd made in her mind.

Again her face grew warm as she thought of her wish to kiss Luke.

"The mountains are beautiful—shades of red and gold in the sunlight, blue black in the moonlight. Wasn't it moonlight you were wishing for?"

Ashley was positive she hadn't wished aloud. "How do you know what I wished for?" she asked.

"I told you. The mountains have magical powers."

"The mountains, maybe. But not you."

Luke leaned forward. His eyes were deep and compelling. "Come with me into the mountains, Ashley."

Ashley closed her eyes and took a step closer to him.

Suddenly she heard her mother out in the hallway. "Have any of you seen Ashley?" Her voice was tight with anxiety. "She was supposed to have been on that last bus."

Ashley ran toward the doorway. She stopped and gave a last look over her shoulder at Luke. "I'm sorry. I wish I could go with you, but . . ."

Luke grinned and gave Ashley a mock salute. "That wish is good enough for me," he said.

That night Ashley went to sleep clutching her lucky stone. As she slept, she dreamed she was walking into the mountains with Luke, climbing the jagged rocks, clinging to rough, broken walls. But when she looked around, Luke wasn't there. She was alone with the mountains, tall and dark, looming overhead and slowly closing in on her. She woke up gasping with fear, her heart racing.

Ashley didn't see Luke before she left for the set, and he wasn't waiting for the bus when she arrived. Where was he? As the thickening clouds grew darker, Ashley's spirits did, too. Why hadn't he come to see her?

"Good sky," the director said.

"Yeah," his assistant answered. "Just right."

But Ashley shivered when she looked up at the clouds. Dark streaks of shadow spread up and down the rocky outcrops of Mount Kinesava, reds and golds suddenly deepening to maroons and grays. The quickly changing light seemed to make faces appear and disappear in the rocks, all of them scowling down at the people who had invaded their valley.

Dusk came quickly, and with it Luke. He suddenly appeared at Ashley's side and took her hand.

"Board your buses," someone called. Actors, extras, and crew began tiredly walking toward the buses.

"Come with me," Luke said to Ashley.

She tried to say no, but the word wouldn't form. Instead she began to walk beside him toward the mountains. But glancing back at the buses, she hesitated. "I can't miss the bus," Ashley said. "There's no other way to get back to St. George."

"You wished to come with me. Remember? Now your wish is coming true," Luke said.

Ashley wanted to tell him that she couldn't, that she really didn't want to. She wanted to ask how he knew about wishes she had never spoken aloud, but she said nothing. His voice was so commanding she followed without complaint.

Luke led her to a rise behind the scraggly-limbed

94

mulberry trees near the small cemetery she had visited before. He stopped under the dark shadows of one of the mulberries and rested one arm around Ashley's shoulders. "We'll stop here for a moment," he said. "It's time for your first wish to come true."

Ashley gulped. She remembered her first wish— that Luke would put an arm around her shoulders and lightly kiss her lips. But how did he know? Her heart pounded. "Who are you?" she whispered.

Frightened by what she didn't understand, she strained to see his face in the growing darkness. Gripping her magic stone, she blurted out, "I wish I knew all about you."

"No!" Luke shouted. He seemed upset. "No more wishes, Ashley!"

"Yes, I need to know!" Ashley cried. "I wish I could see you exactly as you are."

A stream of moonlight burst through the clouds, and Ashley lifted her face.

There, directly in front of her, was a bleached skull with dead hollows where the eyes should have been. A few patches of dark hair still clung to what remained of the scalp.

"As . . . I . . . am," a scratchy voice echoed.

A bony hand clutched her shoulder as the skull came closer.

Too terrified to scream, Ashley jerked away. She tried to run but tripped over tangled tree roots.

The skeleton came forward. It bent over her. "Wishes can come true," the voice rasped.

Whimpering, trying to scramble away, Ashley reached into her pocket for the stone. It had performed magic, but not the kind she wanted. Even though the stone burned her fingers, she clung to it, holding it up so that the skeleton could see it. "I wish I had never met you!" she shouted at the skull.

With all her strength Ashley threw the stone into the darkness.

With a thump that knocked her breath away, she suddenly found herself in the hallway of the St. George Motel. Mrs. Blanton stood beside her, peering into her face.

"Are you all right, girl?" Mrs. Blanton asked. "I didn't mean to run right into you."

Ashley leaned against the door frame of the prop room and breathed deeply, trying to steady herself. "I'm all right," she said.

"Which way are you heading?"

For a moment Ashley struggled to remember. "I—I saw the open door and all the movie props inside the room. I think I was going inside to take a look."

"Not everything in there belongs to the movie folk," Mrs. Blanton said. She squeezed into the doorway next to Ashley and pointed to the photo on the far wall. "That's a picture of my little brother, Luke. It's about all I have left to remind me of him. He was a wild boy, always playing pranks that upset some of the neighbors around here. He wasn't a mean kid. He just liked to have fun. He liked excitement and always wanted something going on. And he liked to share the fun because he hated to be by himself. But one day when he was seventeen, he came home with a weird-looking stone. Looked just like an eye, it did. He told us he had discovered ancient mysticism."

She sighed. "Soon after that, Luke went into the mountains alone and didn't return. His body was never found."

"I'm sorry," Ashley said.

"I still ache for him," Mrs. Blanton went on. "To be alone, to die alone. Luke hated to be alone."

Mrs. Blanton cleared her throat and dabbed at her eyes. With a last look at Luke's photograph, she turned and walked toward the motel office.

Ashley stood in the doorway a moment, staring at the boy in the photograph. High cheekbones, a strong, square chin, dark eyes that seemed to stare right into her own. Too bad he had disappeared. He was certainly good-looking enough to have been a movie star.

As she shoved her hands into her pockets, Ashley was surprised that her new magic stone was no longer there. What had she done with it? She must have dropped it somewhere.

Oh well, it doesn't matter, Ashley decided. After all, it wasn't really magic; it was only a stone.

GRAFTON, UTAH

In 1861 Mormon colonists left Salt Lake City to settle in southern Utah. Some of them established their homes on land close to the Virgin River under a rugged, majestic mountain known as Kinesava. The leader of the Mormon church, Brigham Young, told the settlers this would be Zion, their homeland. This is how Kinesava and more than 146,000 acres of wild, colorful, massive rock formations received the name they have today. Zion was established as a national park in 1919.

Nothing has been recorded to tell us how the town of Grafton was named, but some believe it was named after one of the original settlers.

The settlers brought with them flocks of sheep

and planted cotton. One colonist, hoping to take part in a new venture—the raising of silkworms—brought mulberry seeds and cuttings to her new home and established a small orchard. The silkworm eggs, imported from Asia, were sprinkled on shredded mulberry leaves from the orchard.

Silk production succeeded in the nearby colonies, but not in Grafton. The settlers were too busy defending themselves against Indian raids and the frequent flooding of the Virgin River to make a success of any of their projects. Even rebuilding the town on higher ground and building levees and canals didn't protect it from the heavy spring floods. Family after family left, until by 1930, Grafton was entirely deserted.

Films such as *Butch Cassidy and the Sundance Kid*, starring Robert Redford and Paul Newman, have been shot in Grafton, but now the remains of the town and its cemetery are inhabited only by memories and ghosts.

The town is privately owned, but it is open to those who wish to explore it.

———————◆———————

To reach Grafton, from Highway 15 out of St. George, drive approximately thirty miles on Highway

9 to Rockville. Then take the old bridge road in Rockville and drive about four miles until you reach the town of Grafton.

To learn more about Grafton, contact the Washington County Travel Bureau, 1835 Convention Center Drive, St. George, Utah 84790, and ask for a copy of its tourist guide.

Web sites:
"Wind in the Sage: A Story of Utah Ghost Towns":
www.kbyu.org/tv/cover-march97.html

"Destinations Utah, Great Ghost Towns of the West":
www.azcentral.com/travel/destinations/
utah/ghostutah.shtml

———◆———

Publications:
Ghost Towns of the West, by Lambert Florin, Promontory Press, New York, 1992, pages 366–369.

Historical Guide to Utah Ghost Towns, by Stephen L. Carr, Zion Books, Salt Lake City, 1972.

BAD MAN FROM BODIE

"I've been hoping you'd soon discover the direction your life might take," Dr. Randall Nelson said to his son, Mike. "When I was your age I had already developed a strong interest in history. You can see where it led me."

Mike took his eyes from the pine forests that bordered the mountain road and looked at his father. He slid down in the passenger seat of his dad's car and groaned. "I'm only eleven, Dad. I've got lots of time to decide what I'm going to be when I grow up."

"Of course you have," Dr. Nelson said, and Mike winced at the deliberate patience in his father's voice. "But these are the years to explore ideas, Mike. That's what you should be doing, instead of spending so much time on television and computer games. Discover new pathways. Search for new thoughts. Look for your purpose and goals in life."

"I thought this was going to be a camping trip—for *fun*," Mike grumbled.

Dr. Nelson threw Mike a quick glance before he looked back at the road. "Oh, it *is*, son. It is. I only thought, since we'd be alone for a while without distractions, we'd have a good chance to discuss your future."

Mike edged up in his seat. His dad had switched to the defensive. Now was the time to get his mind going on a completely different track. "Tell me about this ghost town where we're going to stop," he said.

Dr. Nelson's eyes brightened, and he smiled. "Bodie," he answered. "What an exciting history Bodie has. Legend has it that in 1859 a Dutchman from New York state, who had come to California looking for gold, shot and wounded a rabbit. The rabbit dropped into a hole, and Mr. Body—Waterman Bill Body—dug into the hole to get the rabbit. What do you suppose he found?"

"The rabbit," Mike answered. He wished his dad would get to the point.

"Gold!" Dr. Nelson said. "He discovered flakes of

gold. However, Mr. Body died a short time later in a snowstorm, so it wasn't until the mid-1870s that gold and silver mining became successful in Bodie."

He chuckled, and Mike asked, "What's so funny?"

"Just an amusing footnote," Dr. Nelson said. "Rumor had it that in the early 1860s a sign painter was hired to paint a sign for Body's Stables. He misspelled 'Body.' Instead of spelling it 'B-O-D-Y,' he printed it as 'B-O-D-I-E,' and the town has been known as Bodie with an 'I-E' ever since."

Mike couldn't believe that story was funny enough to make his dad laugh. He sighed, then asked, "How long do we have to be in Bodie before we can leave for our camping trip in Yosemite?"

"Only long enough for me to get the information I'm after," Dr. Nelson replied.

"How long is that?"

"I can't be exact."

Mike turned and studied his father. "Dad," he said, "we *are* going camping in Yosemite, aren't we?"

Dr. Nelson kept his eyes on the unpaved road. "Of course. That's what I said we'd do, but remember, I did tell you that first I needed to do some research in Bodie for the lecture I'm preparing. We'll stay in a Bridgeport motel—it's fairly near Bodie—for just a night or two before we head to Yosemite."

Mike sighed. He should have known they'd be in Bodie a lot longer than a few hours. As Mike's mother often reminded him, his father, a highly respected professor of history at California State University in Sacramento, was dedicated to his work.

As far as Mike was concerned, his father didn't live in the twenty-first century. He lived somewhere in California back in the 1800s—his period of specialization—and he only came out for meals, family birthdays, holidays, and an occasional baseball game.

Dr. Nelson slowed the van and drove into a parking lot next to the visitors' center. "The Department of Parks and Recreation maintains what's left of Bodie as a California State Park," he said. "There's a nice little museum in the visitors' center, and you can tour the remaining buildings. You'll find a hotel, the Odd Fellows Hall, and—"

"Dad! Enough history, okay?" Mike said. He opened the car door and climbed out, impatient to stand up and stretch.

Dr. Nelson shook his head in bewilderment as he joined Mike. "I can't understand why you aren't excited about history, Mike. Just look around you. This was once an active town that was filled with prospectors and miners and bandits and gamblers and dance hall girls and—"

"Bye, Dad!" Mike said. He'd had enough. Bypassing the visitors' center, where his father was headed, he wandered alone down Bodie's main street. No one was in sight—probably because it was so late in the day.

A few beat-up and weathered wooden buildings faced the main street, with gaps between them like missing teeth. A scattering of buildings lay beyond, where the other streets of the town must have been. It was hard for Mike to imagine anybody wanting to work and live in a dump like this.

Eventually he strolled up to the Boot Hill cemetery, on a hill south of the town. But when he saw his father busily copying names and dates from the array of tombstones, he quickly turned away. The last thing he wanted was to hear his dad going on and on about some of the people buried there and how they'd died.

A short, thin branch lay on the path to the main street. Mike picked it up, along with a small, rounded stone the size of a golf ball. Aiming for a hole in the dirt road ahead, Mike gently hit the stone with the branch and made his putt.

"Hey, pretty good," he said.

He hit the stone over and over again, until it skittered into a ragged patch of weeds that lay between the remains of two wooden buildings on the main street.

Mike knew he had plenty of time to kill until his dad would be ready to leave, so he began to hunt for the stone.

It was easy to find. It lay in a depression just beyond a tangled clump of weeds. The ground wasn't hard packed. It was soft and still a little damp, as if there had been a recent rain.

With the end of his stick Mike began to dig. He remembered his father's story about how Bill Body had discovered gold flakes in a rabbit hole. Who knew what he would find?

Only a short way into the ground, his stick hit something hard, and he used his fingers to dig it up. Knocking the dirt away, he was surprised to see in the palm of his hand a thin white bone, little more than an inch long.

His first thought was that someone had dumped the garbage from his lunch, but he knew almost immediately that he was wrong. This wasn't a chicken bone. It looked more like the pictures of human bones he'd seen in health class. He held it up, matching it to his hand. It had to be part of a finger—a human bone.

Mike dropped the bone into the pocket of his jeans and dug in the hole some more. What if he found a whole body? Would there be a reward? Would they put his picture in the newspaper?

Mike dug a sizable hole, but his work didn't turn up a thing. All he had was one small finger bone. The mystery nagged him. How had the bone gotten there? Who had lost part of a finger? And what had happened to the rest of him?

There were no answers, and Mike wasn't planning on staying in Bodie long enough to try to find any. He sighed and wished they could head for Yosemite soon. He sat on the steps of the visitors' center and yawned, waiting for his father.

When Dr. Nelson arrived he smiled at Mike with satisfaction. "I'm getting even more material than I'd hoped for," he said. "Come on, hop in the car. It's close to five-thirty, so you must be getting hungry."

It wasn't until they had left the gravel road and picked up speed that Dr. Nelson asked, "How did you like the museum?"

"I didn't go to the museum," Mike said.

He caught the flash of disappointment on his father's face. "They present some very interesting relics," Dr. Nelson said. "For example, there are some of the remnants of the miners' lives—their tools and the equipment they used in their homes."

"That kind of stuff doesn't really interest me," Mike answered.

Dr. Nelson thought a minute, then suggested,

"You might want to talk to one of the rangers who staff the park. They could tell you some interesting stories about the people who once lived in Bodie."

Mike's only answer was a shrug.

He could see his dad struggling to come up with the right thing to say. Finally Dr. Nelson smiled. "I think the best thing for us to do is check into the motel and get some dinner. How about it, Mike?"

"Sure," Mike said.

They found a good diner, and later they watched a movie on the TV in their motel room. Mike forgot all about the bone in his pocket.

But in the middle of the night he awoke, his feet cramped because something heavy had settled on them.

In the dim light coming from the crack under the door and the hotel's neon light shining between the drapes, Mike saw a dark figure on the end of his bed. It was sitting on him.

"Dad? Is that you?" he whispered, but he realized it couldn't be his father. He could hear his dad's soft, rhythmic snoring coming from the other bed.

Mike's heart began to pound. He tried to sit up, but whoever was on his feet wasn't about to let him move. "Who are you?" Mike whispered.

The figure leaned closer, grinning at Mike. "Take a good look at me," he said.

Greasy strands of hair fell to his shoulders from under a dirty felt hat. The skin on his nose was red and blotchy, his teeth were stained, and his breath stank. "I was known far and wide as the Bad Man from Bodie," he said. "I was the baddest of the bad. I was the roughest and toughest of them all—and there were plenty of bad ones in Bodie, let me tell you."

Mike shivered with fright, but he managed to ask, "What do you want, Bad Man from Bodie? What are you doing here?"

"You can call me Jack," the man said, adding smugly, "I was also known as Rough and Tumble Jack."

Again Mike tried unsuccessfully to pull his feet out from under Jack. "Why are you here?" he asked.

Jack slowly held up his left hand, spreading out his fingers. The top third of his index finger was missing, and the second knuckle down was a shattered, bloody mess.

"One night a dirty, lily-livered coward called me a liar—right there in the saloon in front of everybody. Challenged me, that's what he did, so we went outside in the street to see who was right. Drew our guns at the same time, all fair and square. My shot shattered that feller's arm, and I thought he'd learned his lesson. But danged if he didn't shoot off the end of my finger."

Mike gulped. "Ouch," he said.

"At the time I didn't know it was gone. Shock, I guess, and there wasn't a moon, so it was too dark outside to see the blood. I went back inside the saloon, ready to brag that I'd put that no-good in his place. Then along he comes with his gun he'd reloaded by holding it between his knees. Shot me right there in the bar and killed me dead."

"Dead?" Mike stared in disbelief.

Jack sighed. "When they put my body in a coffin, nobody noticed that part of my finger was missing. Or if they noticed, they didn't care." He sighed again and added, "Only a couple of folks came to the funeral. The blacksmith's wife was there. Somewhat unkindly, she said she could rest a lot easier makin' sure I was dead and gone far away from Bodie. At least Mad Molly showed up and shed a few tears. A might tawdry Molly was, but she had a kind heart."

The blacksmith's wife had the right idea. Mike, too, wished Jack had gone far away from Bodie.

Jack suddenly stopped reminiscing and waggled his hand in Mike's face. "You've got my finger, and I want it," he growled.

"You can have it," Mike said eagerly. "I mean, you can have what's left of it. Part is missing—like the flesh and the blood and the dirty fingernail. All I have is the bone, and it's in the pocket of my jeans."

Jack looked startled. Furtively he examined his fingernails, then shook his head. "You had no call to point out the lack of a manicure. They weren't to be had in the likes of Bodie. The bone's all I want."

"Then take it!" Mike cried.

"No. It's not that easy," Jack snapped. He scowled at Mike. "What I need you to do is—"

The bedside light flipped on. Dr. Nelson squinted at Mike, then put on his glasses to look at him more closely. "You were talking in your sleep, son. You yelled something. Were you having a bad dream?" he asked.

Mike stared down at the end of his bed. Jack had vanished. "Yeah, I guess," he answered. Then he sat up in bed. "Dad," he said, "you told me that the rangers at Bodie would know all about the people who lived there. Could I talk to them tomorrow? Will they be able to answer my questions?"

Dr. Nelson's eyes opened wide in pleased surprise. "Of course they will. May I ask what you have in mind?"

Mike wasn't about to tell his father about the bone he had found or the visit by the Bad Man from Bodie. But he had to give him some kind of explanation. "All of a sudden I kinda have this interest in history, Dad," he said.

"Wonderful, Mike!" Dr. Nelson beamed. "You don't know how much that pleases me." He glanced at the clock, then reached for the light. "It's two-sixteen A.M., so we have four hours and forty-four minutes left to sleep. Let's make the most of it."

At nine-thirty the next morning Mike's father led him into Bodie's Miners' Union Hall, which had been turned into a visitors' center. They passed a large bulletin board, which displayed letters and drawings from kids who had visited Bodie, and went to the desk. There Dr. Nelson introduced Mike to a ranger named Susan. Giving Mike another happy smile, Dr. Nelson left to continue his own research.

"Your father said you had some questions," Susan said. "Anything in particular you want to know?"

"Yes," Mike said. "Have you ever heard of somebody who called himself the Bad Man from Bodie? His real name was Jack."

Susan smiled. "A lot of outlaws liked to claim that they were the Bad Man from Bodie, but I bet you're talking about Rough and Tumble Jack," she said. "He was a real tough character. There's no telling how many men he killed before someone shot and killed him back in 1878."

Mike gulped. He didn't want anything to do with a murderer. The sooner he could give Jack his bone,

113

the better. He wished his dad hadn't interrupted before Jack had spelled out exactly what it was he wanted Mike to do. "Did everybody call him the Bad Man from Bodie?" Mike asked Susan.

"As I understand it, Rough and Tumble Jack was what he was usually called, although you could certainly say that Jack was first to fit the title of the Bad Man from Bodie.

"There were plenty of bad men from Bodie during the late 1870s and early 1880s. Any one of them could have been known by that name, and some of them liked to claim it. Over and over, outlaws robbed the Concord stagecoaches that carried gold and silver bullion through the canyon to Aurora, and there were so many shootings that took place in Bodie, I doubt if anyone bothered to count them."

Mike interrupted. "Do you have a picture of Jack?"

"No, I don't. Sorry."

"Some of his stuff?"

"Stuff? No. Nothing in our museum collection has any tie to Rough and Tumble Jack."

Mike thought a moment. "Can you tell me this about Jack—was he buried here in Boot Hill?"

"Yes, he was," Susan answered.

Mike remembered Jack's description of his burial. "With only Mad Molly to cry at his funeral," he said.

Susan raised an eyebrow. "You must have read something I didn't. Who's Mad Molly?"

"A citizen of Bodie," Mike said quickly. He couldn't tell anybody about Jack's visit. "I'm going to—to look at some of the buildings now," he said. "Thanks for the information."

"Check that large bulletin board near the door," Susan suggested. "Sometimes the kids who write to us include what they've learned in class about our historical characters. I don't remember anything written about Rough and Tumble Jack, but it wouldn't hurt to check."

Mike thanked Susan and walked to the board to have a look. Most of the postings were letters from kids who'd visited on school tours. Some wrote about the schoolhouse and the Boot Hill cemetery. Some had illustrated their letters with drawings, and a few had taped things to the letters: wildflowers, a horse made out of Popsicle sticks, a row of tiny cardboard tombstones.

Suddenly Mike saw the words "Bad Men from Bodie," and he bent to read the letter. There was another letter tacked nearby. Both writers told about the rush of bad guys to Bodie to rob the stagecoaches carrying gold from Bodie to Aurora; the claim jumpers, who stole each other's mining property; and the gunslingers wanted by the law. Neither of the letters mentioned Rough and Tumble Jack, who didn't seem to be nearly as famous—or infamous—as he himself thought.

Mike left the center and strolled down the street, past a few scattered groups of visitors. Looking for somewhere to hang out, Mike turned on King Street and walked into a livery stable.

"There you be," a deep voice growled.

Far back in the shadows Mike saw Jack sitting on a bale of hay. Jack pushed his grimy hat from his forehead and held up his mangled left hand. "I want my bone," he said. "You wouldn't deny me the right to be all in one piece, would you?"

Mike pulled the bone from his pocket and held it out. "Here it is. You can have it. Right now."

"Just what am I supposed to do with it?"

"Well, you said—"

"*You* have to bury it. I can't."

"Okay," Mike said. He sighed with relief. All he had to do was put the bone back into the hole where he'd found it and cover it with dirt.

"It has to be buried in the cemetery," Jack said.

"Well . . . okay."

"With the rest of my body."

Mike gasped. "How am I going to do that?"

"Simple," Jack said. "You dig up my coffin, put my finger bone in with the rest of my bones, and bury the coffin again."

"I can't," Mike said.

Jack sniffed and looked down his nose. "When I was a lad, I was taught never to say 'can't.' "

"Be reasonable," Mike said. "I'm just a kid. How am I going to dig up your coffin?"

"With a shovel."

Mike shook his head and took a step back. "No way," he said.

Jack's face grew dark. He scowled. He glowered. "I forgot to say what I should have said—you bury it right . . . or else."

Mike slowly took another step back. "Or else what?"

Now Jack grinned wickedly. "You don't want to find out."

Mike backed to the edge of the stable door; it pressed against his back. "I'll think about it," he shouted, and dashed out of the stables.

He found his father in the graveyard, still copying information from the tombstones. Dr. Nelson looked up at Mike in surprise, as if he wondered for a moment just who Mike was and what he was doing there.

He seemed suddenly to remember, and his eyes lit up with pleasure. "Did you find the answers to your questions, son?" he asked.

"Yes, but now I have another question that you can answer," Mike said. "How do you get somebody who's been buried in a cemetery dug up and then buried again?"

Dr. Nelson dropped his pencil. "Is this a hypothetical question?" he asked.

"No, the guy's really dead," Mike said.

"Suppose you tell me why . . ."

Mike tried to think of a good excuse. Remembering something he'd heard on a television show, he answered, "I'm interested in—uh—forensic science. You said to explore ideas, Dad. Well, right now I'd like to see some old bones. Do you think we could dig up some old bones, so I could see what they were like?"

Dr. Nelson's mouth opened and closed a couple of times before he could speak. "Mike," he said, "I appreciate this newfound interest of yours. In fact, I applaud your ingenuity. However, some actions just aren't feasible, and exhuming a body is one of them. Do you understand?"

"Everything except the big words," Mike said. "But I get what you mean. The answer is no."

"Correct," Dr. Nelson said. He cocked his head

and studied Mike. "There is a direct correlation between the study of history and forensic paleontology. Archaeology, as well. You know—the study of mankind through what has been left behind. Many of the earth sciences are linked. Would you like me to tell you more about it, son?"

"Sure, Dad," Mike said, "but later. Okay? I've got stuff to do."

He ran down the route he had taken, stopping when he got to a large trash bin. Jack had no right to make him bury that finger bone. It wasn't Mike's fault that Jack hadn't kept track of his finger. Unearthing Jack's coffin would be impossible. The more he thought about Jack's demands, the angrier Mike got.

Once again he pulled the bone from his pocket. This time he dropped it into the trash.

"You shouldn't have done that." A raspy voice spoke behind him.

Mike whirled around to see Jack leaning against a nearby post. "I can't dig up your body!" Mike insisted.

Jack scowled. His face grew even darker and more sinister. "I hope you don't mind missing your sleep," he said. "Until you do the right thing by my finger bone, you and I are going to spend a lot of time together."

Mike sighed and turned back to the trash bin. Leaning into it, he pulled out sticky soft-drink cups, greasy paper, and used tissues, searching more and more frantically for the bone.

He gave a sigh of relief as his fingers touched the bone and closed tightly around it.

"Mike? What in the world are you doing, son?" he heard his father ask.

Mike straightened. He slipped the bone into his pocket and brushed himself off. "I was doing a little archaeology, Dad. You know—studying people by what they leave behind."

"That's not quite—" Dr. Nelson began.

But Mike hurried to return the trash to the bin. "I'm still exploring directions, Dad," he said.

Dr. Nelson glanced at his watch. "I'm going to the visitors' center, Mike. I should finish my work within the next twenty minutes or so. Then we'll drive directly to Yosemite."

"Great," Mike said, but he had a hard time sounding enthusiastic. He had to figure out what to do with this bone.

He sat under the shade of the tree against which Jack had leaned. Mike frowned as he thought about Jack. Even though he'd been the baddest of the bad, probably nobody knew it. An idea began to come to him.

"Jack?" he asked quietly.

"Right here," Jack said, and appeared. His face was uncomfortably close to Mike, who winced at Jack's blast of bad breath. "I told you I'd be haunting your very footsteps. I'd be—"

"You might as well," Mike said. "At least I know who you are. None of the other visitors to Bodie will ever learn anything about you."

Jack drew back, startled. "What? Are you daft? Not know about Rough and Tumble Jack, the Bad Man from Bodie?"

Mike looked Jack straight in his bloodshot eyes and said, "There's not a thing in the museum about you." He shrugged. "I suppose you already know that a whole bunch of stagecoach bandits, claim jumpers, and gunslingers have claimed the name 'Bad Man from Bodie.' "

Jack shook with anger, disappearing for a moment. But he returned, his face drawn and somewhat pale. "That can't be," he said. "*I'm* the Bad Man from Bodie. I belong in that museum. The rangers can't leave me out!"

"It's not the rangers' fault," Mike explained. "You didn't leave anything behind that they can put in their exhibit, and none of the kids who've visited Bodie have written about you."

Mike waited quietly. He watched Jack scowl and fume, then suddenly pause as the idea struck him. "I did so leave something behind," Jack said in wonder. "I left part of my finger."

Mike pretended to be surprised. "Hey! That's right."

"And you can write, can't you?"

Mike nodded.

Jack, whose breath was worse than ever, leaned toward Mike. Trying not to breathe, Mike scrunched up his nose. "So do it!" Jack shouted. "Hurry up. Write something about me to put in the museum."

Mike didn't move. He looked at Jack a long moment. "If I do, will you leave me alone? Will you get out of my life forever?"

"It's a deal," Jack said. "Some people may not consider me an honest man in certain ways, but to me a deal is a deal, and I'll honor it." His lip curled up in a sneer. "Besides, I'll be as glad to get rid of you as you'll be to get rid of me. You don't have much of a life—at least by my standards."

"Okay," Mike said. "Wait here. I'll be right back."

He quickly found his father and asked for a pen and a sheet of paper. "I want to write something about Bodie to post on the museum's bulletin board," Mike explained.

Dr. Nelson smiled broadly. "I'm delighted, son," he said as he handed him the paper and pen. "What is your topic?"

Mike didn't hesitate. "The original Bad Man from Bodie," he said. He left his father looking puzzled but happy.

At the visitors' center, it didn't take long for Mike to write what he had in mind. At the top of the paper he sketched Jack's scowling face, and at the bottom he fastened the bone with a piece of Scotch tape from a roll on the ranger's desk. Then he returned to Jack and held up the paper.

Jack studied it for a moment, then said, "So that's what I look like. I never had much call to look in a mirror. Never had a mirror, for that matter."

It was easy to see that Jack liked his portrait, but Mike asked, "What about what I wrote? Is that okay?"

Jack cleared his throat. "I never had much need to learn to read, neither. You read it to me."

"Okay," Mike said. "I wrote it sort of like a Wanted poster. The big letters say, 'WANTED: ROUGH AND TUMBLE JACK, THE ORIGINAL BAD MAN FROM BODIE.' Then it says, 'Meaner than mean, badder than bad, armed and dangerous.' And down at the bottom I wrote, 'The Bad Man from Bodie's authentic fingertip. Do not touch.'"

Jack wiped his eyes and blew his nose on his sleeve.

"That's downright beautiful," he said. "I have just one question. What does *authentic* mean?"

"My dad uses that word a lot," Mike answered. "It means *real,* but it sounds more official."

"I never was on a Wanted poster before," Jack said. He blew his nose again. "Go ahead. Put it in the museum."

Hesitating, Mike asked, "And you'll never bother me again?"

"Never."

Mike ran to the museum and tacked his poster at the top of the bulletin board. He had fulfilled his promise to Jack, and he'd found a place in the museum for the bone—at least for the present.

"Mike?" he heard his father call. "Are you ready to leave?"

"Right away, Dad," Mike said. He walked out the door whistling. He and his father were going camping in Yosemite, and the Bad Man from Bodie was going to remain in Bodie. As Rough and Tumble Jack had said, "A deal is a deal."

BODIE, CALIFORNIA

An altitude of well over eight thousand feet and frequent snowstorms made Bodie, California, a difficult place in which to prospect for gold. But in 1878, the success of the Bodie Mine, which yielded $600,000 in gold ore in just one month, drew prospectors and miners from all over the West. In four years the Bodie Mine, and other mines around it, gave up well over $25 million worth of gold and silver ore.

Adventurers, gamblers, grocers, barbers, and bankers came, too, and a thriving town was built.

But Bodie was rough and tough, and its citizens bragged about it. With the exception of the few honest people in town, they jumped each other's claims, robbed stages, and engaged in deadly fights between unions. Some of them were known for shooting with little provocation, and vigilante committees did little or nothing to bring order to the town.

The stage carrying gold and silver bullion out of Bodie was robbed regularly, and Bodie's many saloons did a booming business.

Many outlaws headquartered in Bodie claimed the title of Bad Man from Bodie, but most historians agree that Rough and Tumble Jack was probably most deserving of that dubious distinction.

The citizens of Bodie were an impulsive lot. In 1879 a committee was formed to pay honor to the remains of Bill Body, buried in a Boot Hill cemetery, and a handsome headstone was ordered for his grave. When it finally arrived, in September of 1881, President James Garfield had just been assassinated. The committee voted to forget Bill Body's memorial and use the stone as a monument to President Garfield instead.

Although close to $75 million worth of gold was removed from Bodie's mines, they began to fail, and in 1883 Bodie mining stocks crashed.

The town rapidly fell into disrepair as its citizens abandoned their houses and rushed to find the next big strike.

In 1932 a fire destroyed two thirds of the town, but

many interesting buildings remain. The town is maintained by the California Department of Parks and Recreation as a California State Park, and rangers are on hand during the summer months to answer questions.

It has been estimated that as much gold remains under Bodie and the area around it as was taken from the mines, but many of the mine shafts have collapsed, and the cost of removing the gold would be more than the gold is worth.

———•———

To reach Bodie, drive six miles south of Bridgeport on California State Highway 270 and take the turnoff to the east that begins as a paved road. Continue for thirteen miles on a dirt road.

To learn more about Bodie, contact the Bodie State Historic Park, P.O. Box 515, Bridgeport, CA 93517. Telephone: (760) 647-6445.

Web sites:
Bodie, State Historic Park, Its Life and Times:
www.redmondwa.com/bodie

Bodie, A Ghost Town That Lives On:
www.yosemitegold.com/yosemite/bodie.html

Publications:

Ghost Towns and Mining Camps of California: A History and Guide, by Remi Nadeau, Crest Publishers, Santa Barbara, California, 1999, pages 202–203 and 228–236.

Bodie—Boom Town of California, by Douglas McDonald, Nevada Publications, Reno, 1988.

Ghost Towns of the West, by Lambert Florin, Promontory Press, New York, 1992, pages 167–168.

TRADE-OFF

Josh Peavy made a last halfhearted sweep with his broom at a corner in Fort Griffin's powder magazine.

Scarcely a speck of dust flew up. Once again he'd done a good job of keeping the old, drafty, sawed-lumber buildings clean, readying them for the new day's group of tourists, who were bound to leave a scattering of litter before moving on.

Helping to keep the fort clean was a boring, lonely job for a ghost, Josh thought. But at least he had a job, and for that he was grateful. There weren't many jobs around an army post that a ghost of only thirteen years could be trusted to do. At least, that's what the ghost of Sergeant Bart Holter had pointed out.

129

Josh sighed. He missed Sergeant Holter. An older ghost, with skin as weathered as pine bark, the sergeant had been strong and tough, yet kind enough to take Josh in hand when he arrived after his fatal accident with an oxcart. The sergeant taught Josh how to survive on his own and had been the closest thing to a parent Josh had known.

Sometimes Josh would watch the families who came to tour Texas's Fort Griffin State Historical Park, and he'd wonder what it would be like to be alive again, to have a mother and a father and be part of a real family. Once, he'd told Sergeant Holter how much he wished—even ached inside—to be a real boy again and have a family to love.

"I don't remember my mother, who died when I was two. And I was ten when my father was killed," he'd said.

After Josh had let the words spill from his heart, he'd wished he hadn't. He'd expected the sergeant to gruffly tell him that nothing could come from wishful thinking.

But instead Sergeant Holter had cocked his head and looked thoughtful. "Bide your time," he'd told Josh. "Be patient. If luck looks your way, some day you may find yourself part of a family."

"How?" Josh had asked.

"Keep your eyes open for the right opportunity for a trade-off," Sergeant Holter had answered. "Luck means being prepared when the right opportunity comes along."

Josh had been puzzled. "What's a trade-off?" he asked.

"It's an even trade between you and someone living. You trade your situation for his."

"You mean I'd become him, and he'd cross over to this side and become me?"

"Only if he asks to make the change."

Josh knew he must have looked as disturbed as he felt, because Sergeant Holter's voice had grown softer as he explained, "Trade-offs don't take place often, but they do happen. You look for someone who's discontented, someone whose body you wouldn't mind inhabiting, and be ready for the trade. No problem. You just have to keep looking for that opportunity and make the most of it."

"But what if after he gets here on this side he doesn't like it and wants to go back?" Josh had asked.

"No going back." Sergeant Holter had shaken his head. "However, if he wants to return to the living, he can keep his eyes and ears open, hoping to make a trade-off with someone else."

Sergeant Holter had smiled, then explained the

ritual that Josh needed to know to make the trade-off happen. "Once the deal is done and payment is made, you must move quickly. Keep your head down and dive directly into the body. Don't wait. Don't hesitate. Don't think about it."

Josh had nodded, intent on what Sergeant Holter had said.

"Just keep in mind," the sergeant had cautioned, "a trade-off has to be a mutual agreement, bought and paid for."

"I will," Josh had answered. Now, resting his chin on his broom, he thought once again about the deep smile lines that crinkled around the sergeant's eyes and gave a sigh. The opportunity had come for Sergeant Holter to take a trade-off and leave the fort, and he'd done it. But that was years ago, and Josh greatly missed his friend.

For a good, long time Josh had watched and waited, remembering what Sergeant Holter had told him, but so far the opportunity for a trade-off hadn't come.

Suddenly a boy about Josh's age stomped into the room, carrying a whiff of the pine-scented breeze with him. "Okay, okay, so now I've seen a powder magazine. Are you happy?" he snarled. He brushed his dark hair out of his eyes and glared at the woman and man who hurried into the room after him.

"Marty Allen Lane!" the woman cried. "Just once—just *once*—can't you cooperate?"

The man kept his eyes on Marty but spoke to his wife. "If Marty would enter into the spirit of this trip, he might be surprised to find he could even enjoy himself."

"Fat chance," Marty mumbled.

"Thirteen." Mrs. Lane sighed and rolled her eyes. She seemed to be speaking to herself. "Everyone told us thirteen was a difficult age, and they were right."

Josh was puzzled. He was thirteen, too, but he had never heard anyone speak of thirteen as being a difficult age. At thirteen a boy helped around the home or farm from sunup to sundown. Maybe he would also have a job or be apprenticed to the blacksmith or the baker to earn extra money for the family while he learned a trade. And if there were a school and teacher nearby, he could look forward to at least another year of study. What was so difficult about that?

A younger boy—Josh guessed he was eight or nine—stumbled over the threshold, steadying himself on the stroller he was pushing. Inside the stroller sat a baby girl about eighteen months old. She smiled at Josh and wiggled her fingers. "Hi," she said.

"Hi," Josh answered, and smiled back.

The other members of the Lane family ignored him, but Josh was used to that. It hadn't taken him long to discover that only babies could see through to the other side. Someone as impolite as Marty Lane—if he could see Josh, too—would probably get scared and start yelling, "Ghost!"

The younger boy looked questioningly from one parent to the other and then to Marty. "Come on, Marty. Let's go," he said. "I want to see the whole fort. I've got to write about it for my report, and I want to get a good grade."

"Get out of here, Sammy. Go see your stupid fort by yourself," Marty said. "You don't need me."

Sammy looked wistful. "They've got a real herd of old Longhorn cattle," he said. "Don't you want to see them, too, Marty?"

"A bunch of cows? Big deal," Marty sneered. "I'm not interested."

"Oh, Marty." His mother sighed with exasperation and patted Sammy's shoulder.

Josh could see the hurt in Sammy's eyes, and he wished he could take a punch at Marty. What a rotten way to treat a little brother. What a rotten way to treat his whole family.

Sammy backed out of the room with the stroller. Mrs. Lane followed, but Mr. Lane paused, scowling at Marty. "Your behavior is unacceptable, son," he said. "For two cents I'd turn the car around and take you straight home."

Marty dove a hand into the pocket of his jeans and came up with two pennies. He smirked as he threw them at his father's feet. "Here's your two cents," he said. "So do it. Let's go."

Mr. Lane's face flushed red with anger, and it took him a moment to calm himself. "We'll leave when we're good and ready," he snapped, and strode from the building.

Marty leaned against the wall and scowled. Josh, amazed at how little regard tourists had for copper pennies, carefully picked up the two coins. He thought of how he once would have used them to buy a loaf of bread or a paper twist filled with candy. He might still make use of them.

Josh trembled with excitement. Could he? Would the opportunity he'd been waiting for actually come? He'd have to plan carefully. He had the coins to buy the trade-off, and he'd learned how to do it from

Sergeant Holter. Quietly Josh placed the coins in a corner of the nearest windowsill, where he hoped Marty wouldn't notice them.

Marty leaned against the rough, wooden boards, intent only on himself. This allowed Josh to study him carefully. Even though they were close to the same age, Marty was at least four inches taller than Josh, and his shoulders were broader. He seemed strong and healthy and capable of a good day's work. But Josh was able to see the anger and bitterness within.

For a few moments Josh considered giving up his hopes for a trade-off, but he had felt the strong love the Lane parents had for their son. He liked Sammy, who obviously needed a brother to care for him, and he smiled as he thought of the baby sister who had greeted him.

Josh made his decision to give the trade-off a try. He took a deep breath, then stared intently at a center point in Marty's forehead. *Calm yourself,* he commanded.

Marty gave a shuddering sigh. "Why doesn't everybody just calm down and leave me alone?" he grumbled.

Josh studied Marty. Was he getting through to him? The key words seemed to be reaching Marty, even if he didn't get the message straight. Before Josh tried to reach Marty again, he reviewed every step of the ritual Sergeant Holter had explained to him.

Mrs. Lane suddenly appeared in the doorway. "Marty," she said, "Sammy's very disappointed that you aren't with us. Won't you come?"

Marty growled, "Everybody's always telling me what to do. All the time. I don't have to take orders."

"I wasn't ordering. I was requesting," Mrs. Lane said. She looked at her son and sighed. "Marty, dear, your family loves you."

"All my family does is bug me. Especially Sammy. Especially you and Dad. You all drive me crazy." He glared up at his mother and said, "I can't wait until I'm old enough to get away."

Josh stood still . . . listening . . . hoping.

Mrs. Lane shook her head, mumbling, "Oh! For two cents, I'd . . ."

"For two cents you'd what?" Marty taunted.

Without another word his mother whirled and stalked out of the building.

Josh took a deep breath as a ray of sunlight touched the pennies on the windowsill. Could he do it? Could he manage it? Silently he picked up the pennies and stood directly in front of Marty, waiting for him to say the words.

137

Marty's lower lip curled out, and he scowled. In a mocking tone of voice he muttered, "For two cents I'd get away from them right this minute and be on my own and never come back."

Josh smiled. Here it was. A mutual agreement. The deal was done. He dropped the two pennies into the pocket of Marty's shirt. "Here's the two cents," he said. "You're paid off. You can go now."

Josh quickly dove into Marty's body. The last trace of Marty was ejected with a whoosh. A flurry of dust flew up at the doorway, whirling outside as it was picked up by the breeze. The room was left in complete silence.

Josh took a couple of deep breaths, delighted at the trade-off. He wasn't worried about Marty. Sooner or later Marty would find someone to teach him the ritual of trade-offs, and by that time his attitude toward the people around him was bound to have improved.

But there was one more thing Josh had to do.

At the edge of the field where the longhorns were kept, Josh found Marty's family leaning on a rail, watching the cattle. He took a deep breath, enjoying the familiar, pungent fragrance of the grass in the hot sunlight.

"Mom . . . Dad?" he said. He liked the way the

language that had been stored in Marty's brain slid across his tongue, and he wasn't afraid to use words that were new to him.

"When the trade-off happens, it will all come natural to you," Sergeant Holter had said, and he'd been right.

"I'm sorry for the way I acted," Josh told the Lanes.

His new father's mouth dropped open, and his new mother's eyes widened with surprise.

"I've been a jerk," Josh said, "and I'm sorry. I'm not going to act that way again. I promise."

Mr. Lane clapped a hand on Josh's shoulder. He gulped, too overcome to speak.

Tears came to Mrs. Lane's eyes, and she whispered, "Oh, Marty, we love you."

"I love you, too, Mom," Josh said. He reached over and ruffled Sammy's hair. "I love you, too, pest," he said, and grinned at the joy on Sammy's face. "What else do you want to show me?"

"They've got a living history program," Sammy shouted. He grabbed Josh's arm and tugged. "It's down at the museum. Come on!"

As Josh left with Sammy, he heard his father ask his mother in a strangled whisper, "What just happened?"

"I don't know," his mother answered. "But it doesn't matter. Just enjoy it."

Josh wished he could tell them, "From now on you'll have a son who will make you happy, and I'll have a real family to love me. Marty . . . well, Marty will be on his own, just as he wanted. Don't worry about the trade-off. We're all going to like it."

He looked around at the other groups of people who were touring the ghost town. Were any of them trade-offs, living in someone else's body? Could be. As Sergeant Holter had told him, "Trade-offs don't take place often, but they do happen."

FORT GRIFFIN, TEXAS

Fort Griffin was located on a military reservation established by the United States Army in July 1867. It was one in a chain of forts designed to protect post–Civil War settlers from attacks by Plains Indians.

On a meadow that lay below the fort, the town of Fort Griffin began as a satellite of the army post. Because of its location on the flat land, it was nicknamed The Flat.

During the 1870s, The Flat had more transients than citizens. It soon became a lawless place, filled with gamblers and fugitives from justice. For a while the commander of Fort Griffin put the town under government control and expelled the troublemakers.

But Shackelford County was established, control of The Flat was taken out of the commander's jurisdiction, and the bad element quickly returned.

Buffalo hunting brought hunters and skinners. And the Western Cattle Trail, which led to Dodge City from Texas, passed close by. Cowboys enjoyed stopping off for a break in a place where they could be as wild as they wanted and had to answer to no one.

Because of The Flat's reputation for lawlessness, gunmen, thieves, and people on the run from the law took refuge in the town. Indians from the nearby Tonkawa tribe were heedlessly sold liquor, and some people in The Flat bragged that it had more saloons than any other town. Murders were frequent, and lynchings were common. Shopkeepers, blacksmiths, barbers, and other working people and their families lived in constant danger.

In 1880 the buffalo hunts ended. In 1881 the military fort was abandoned, and the newly constructed railroad bypassed Fort Griffin to go through Albany. As a result The Flat was soon deserted.

Although there is nothing left of The Flat but the abandoned stone Fort Griffin school, the fort itself has been proclaimed a Texas State Historical Park. Some of the ruins have been restored or partly

restored and are open to visitors. Occasionally historical reenactments are held.

———•———

To reach Fort Griffin, travel fifteen miles north of
Albany, Texas, on U.S. Highway 283.

To learn more about Fort Griffin, contact Texas
Parks & Wildlife, 4200 Smith School Road, Austin,
TX 78744, or Fort Griffin State Historical Park,
1701 North U.S. Highway 283, Albany, TX 76430.
Telephone: (915) 762-3592.

Web site: Fort Griffin State Historical Park:
www.tpwd.state.tx.us/park/fortgrif/fortgrif.htm

———•———

Publications:
Ghost Towns of Texas, by T. Lindsay Baker,
University of Oklahoma Press, Norman, 1986, pages
44–48.

*A Texas Frontier: The Clear Fork Country and Fort
Griffin, 1849–1887,* by Ty Cashion, University of
Oklahoma Press, Norman, 1997.

Exploring a Ghost Town

While some ghost towns have been preserved and some have even become places of entertainment, there are many more lonely, deserted, out-of-the way places to discover.

Although the West, with its played-out silver and gold mines, is famous for its ghost towns, these clusters of decaying buildings where people no longer live and work can sometimes be found in other parts of the United States.

If you are interested in finding out about a ghost town in the state in which you live, it's not hard to do.

You might start by asking your librarian for help. Perhaps someone has written a book or a magazine article about a nearby ghost town, and your librarian can help you find it.

The librarian can also help you locate the addresses of your state's chamber of commerce and tourist bureau—even a local historical preservation society, if there is one. If you write to the directors of these organizations and ask them for ghost town information, you should get some interesting material.

When you find a town to explore, find out who

owns the property. If the town is on private land, you'll need to request permission to visit.

Before you visit, read as much as you can about the history of the town so you'll know why people once lived there and why they left.

Never go to the town alone; ask adults to take you there. Your safety is important, and you do not want to be alone in case you come across dangerous spots you haven't expected. In abandoned towns old wooden sidewalks and flooring can break under your feet, and if you leave the roads, you'll need to watch out for open water wells or mine shafts.

A slogan used by ghost town explorers—and there are many such investigators—is "Don't touch. Don't take." While you're exploring, remember you are visiting a part of history, which others may enjoy visiting, too. Souvenir-hunters can quickly destroy what little is left of a ghost town.

When you go exploring, take a camera. You can create a pictorial journal. Include as much information as you can find and describe your own experience in the ghost town. Donate the journal to your library for others to research, or to just read and enjoy.

Perhaps while you're visiting your ghost town,

you'll meet someone who seems a little other-worldly . . . or feel a puff of air against your cheek when there is no wind . . . or glimpse a quick movement, though no one is there . . . or hear what seems to be a whisper . . .

Ghosts? Maybe. But you'll know what to do.
Won't you?

ABOUT THE AUTHOR

JOAN LOWERY NIXON has been called the grande dame of young adult mysteries and is the author of more than a hundred books for young readers, including *Nobody's There; Who Are You?; The Haunting; Murdered, My Sweet; Don't Scream; Spirit Seeker; Shadowmaker; Secret, Silent Screams; A Candidate for Murder; Whispers from the Dead;* and the middle-grade novel *Search for the Shadowman.* Joan Lowery Nixon was the 1997 president of the Mystery Writers of America and is the only four-time winner of the Edgar Allan Poe Best Juvenile Mystery Award. She received the award for *The Kidnapping of Christina Lattimore, The Séance, The Name of the Game Was Murder,* and *The Other Side of Dark,* which was also a winner of the California Young Reader Medal. Her historical fiction includes the award-winning series The Orphan Train Adventures.

Joan Lowery Nixon lives in Houston with her husband.